NOTHING BUT THE WILLOWS

& OTHER THINGS THAT ARE NOT THERE

J.D. BUFFINGTON

NOTHING BUT THE WILLOWS & OTHER THINGS THAT ARE NOT THERE / J.D. BUFFINGTON

Standing 8 Count Publications 2024

Cover art, THE WATCHER, by Stina Patton.

Warning Cry, The Shadow on Pitch, and The Last Tree originally published by the NoSleep Podcast from Creative Reason Media

Camping originally published in Myths, Monsters, Mutations from JayHenge Publishing

Print ISBN: 979-8-9913878-0-4

Contents

Introduction

In this collection, you will find a lot of death and sadness. Some of it is grief for a lost loved one. Some of it is terror at reality being ripped away. And some of it, even for the monsters, is lonely. However, is any of it really there? I find myself writing about loss quite a bit and questioning the nature of being in something so ephemeral as reality. We can pick and choose what to believe and bury our heads deep to hear nary another word. Or we can be overwhelmed with a deluge of information readily available for imbibing. Both, however, can drive us mad. These stories are about learning too much, too suddenly, about something in our periphery. The margins of reality are filled with things we do not want to look at directly. That doesn't mean they don't see us, and seeing may be all there is to believing. But, who believes in whom, and whose reality does it make true?

Gratitude

Several of the following stories were helped along and developed with the guidance of amazing creators. Teresa Ardrey, Sarah Bredeman, Jon Padgett, Chris Ruppert, Jessica Schmeidler, Oli White, and editors of publications who provided constructive feedback in response to submissions; all provided valuable insight and inspiration. Thank you.

And of course, for my mother, Irene, always.

NOTHING BUT THE WILLOWS

THW

There is no such thing as ghosts. No ghosts—no question. Not a thing. For all the evidence to the contrary, nothing stands up to logical deduction. The supernatural can be naturally explained. There are no ghosts, no haunted houses or objects, and no contacting the living from beyond the grave.

I should know: I'm a ghost.

I am certain there is an explanation for why I remain, bound to this Earth, a curse upon the woman who took my life. It's a roundabout sort of argument that we get into regularly. I protest my existence. She points out I exist. I concede with the caveat there is an explanation we haven't figured out. Unable to do research on my own, I goad her into looking into it on occasion, but she is more resigned to her haunting than I am to my continued, unexplained existence.

I found myself attached to her as I awoke from death, a chick imprinting upon hatching. I recognized her. The inebriated woman who slurred her way through karaoke, providing more entertainment than she intended and more nuisance than she could be aware. She must have left following me and my friends. She plowed into the back of my car at a stop sign, I snapped my neck against the steering wheel, the airbag failing to deploy.

I was the only one to lose my life. I could not assure my friends and family that I am a ghost, that an afterlife—of sorts—exists. I am imprisoned by proximity to Stacey and only she can see me.

If I have found any silver lining in being forced to haunt my killer, she has committed to sticking to her limits. I'm a more constant companion than any sponsor could offer. The flipside of that being, I am *constantly* around her. Her ability to grieve and "move on" from her crime burgeoning on impossible.

At first, Stacey denied it as heavily as I did. We screamed at each other. Me in anger. Her in fear. Then vice versa. I could not help crawling into the police car with her. Shouting became tears when no one else would respond to me and no one believed her that I was there.

I was with her as she journeyed through the court system. She plead guilty. Given the lack of a criminal record, her speed in the incident less a contributing factor than the failure of my car in the accident, she served a little over a year in prison.

Though I may be a woman myself, there was a period of adjustment for us both as she had to bathe and relieve herself with me always present. Being in prison, we both had to adjust to seeing a *lot*.

She was in prison, but she was also being haunted. I was both in prison and only had her. There was plenty of terror and stress between us early on. I didn't have to jump or say "boo" to scare her. Waking up with me there, she was reminded of the accident all over again. Sometimes she woke with screams that only increased as nightmare gave way to nightmarish "reality." Others, it was sobbing until she could force herself to get up.

Meanwhile, I had to learn how to be a ghost. I learned that I did not occupy something we came to refer to as "living space." I could lean on walls and sit in chairs but couldn't manipulate anything. Everything is immobile to me. I do not take up space and cannot interrupt objects in motion.

Sitting in the mess hall across the table from her, someone would sit in my same spot. She would see us both, superimposed. Disturbing for her, hilarious for me. I could feel nothing nor see their insides like an MRI.

I can't intentionally walk through walls, but nothing can keep me from my limited orbit around Stacey. I will pass through physical objects if they separate us. I don't get wet. I do not sleep. I have bouts of emotion. I retain a memory of both my life and this un-life.

However, in my resting state, I am pleasantly content.

When she sleeps, time is not boring. I am not fraught with existential loneliness. I am sitting at that stop sign, waiting for a car to cross the intersection, looking at willows growing too close to the signs. Not interacting with Stacey, I am perpetually the last moment in my life. It's not the worst, but I imagine if this is the nature of everyone's afterlife—the possibilities...

The topic of her contacting my family and friends to pass on a supernatural message was discussed frequently, but I forbade it on account of ghosts not existing. Even if my family believed in that sort of thing, who was to say Stacey *wasn't* mad and delivering false hope? The outside world would view at as sick harassment. I wouldn't have it and she gave up trying. We bordered on friendly after a year in prison.

I witnessed how her life was ruined through the accident. Getting jobs became more difficult, even as I tried being her secret coach. Not that I haven't held it all over her head in times of irritation.

"You need to get out." I've told her on numerous occasions. "The air tastes sour when you're depressed. Call Mark. You know he's not doing anything."

"Go out and do *what*?" she moans every time.

"Sit and stare at a wall with each other." I suggest. "Better than stinking up this place all by yourself."

"I've got you." She says without looking at me.

"I'm not real. I'm not here. You're talking to yourself."

"Reasons I *shouldn't* bother Mark—or anyone else." Stacey says. "I'll keep my crazy to myself and watch movies at home."

We've watched all 12 movies she owns so many times that we can recite them from front to back with the TV on mute. That was fun once. I continue to torture her in my own ways, too, though.

I can only influence her senses. My preferred method of exacting spiritual vengeance is to sing to her. I find delicious irony in the fact that the person I was set to haunt with my eternal presence was the drunk karaoke girl.

I sing all manner of songs, making up medleys on the fly or improvising words to fit a situation. Early on, I didn't let her sleep. I was worse than a song stuck in her head because she could actually hear me.

She would need to concentrate on a task, I would sing. She would try to carry on a conversation, I would carry on a tune. When she tried to medicate me away by seeing a psychiatrist while in prison, I would sing in goofy voices, claiming her drugs messed with my abilities. The singing may have been self-therapy.

Alas, she outwitted me in the end. Of those 12 movies she owns, 8 feature princesses and song and dance numbers. She beat me at my own game. We started singing together, until I was bored of singing, then she would sing at me. I forget who haunts who.

"Let's go sing!"

She shudders. Singing in *public*, even thinking of it, reminds her of that night more than me or booze. My insistences have worn her down, and my presence is something separate to the night she killed me. She knows a life ended because she messed up. She didn't know me before. I could be a figment of her imagination that she is more comfortable with than the truth of her own past. I don't apologize, but I do feel sorry—sometimes.

"No, for real," I say. "Call Mark, have him pick you up. We'll go to Morrison's and you'll sing. It'll help. *I'll* help."

"I do like when you harmonize." She smiles, still without looking at me. "But if I call Mark, you must promise to sit in the backseat. I hate it when you sit in the same place as people, it's very unsettling."

"It's funny and if I make you laugh, he thinks you're having a good time. You both like each other, I don't know why you don't just do it already."

"Perv."

"You had no problems performing with Felix a year ago…if anyone's a pervert…"

She throws a pillow at me and laughs, but of course it does nothing as it sails through the room. I've learned not to flinch in my current state.

"Are you going to call him?" I ask, more urging than confirming.

"Fine."

❦❧

Sitting on her stoop, waiting for Mark to arrive, I try to coax an alley cat from between the apartment buildings to come closer. Other people can't see me, but animals, it seems, look at me on occasion. I like to think they do, anyway.

"It won't come." She says.

"Maybe you could do with a pet; they help with the blues, you know? Petting a cat releases endorphins or dopamine or something."

"Oxytocin."

"Whatever."

"Animals don't like you."

"Thanks." I say, ignoring her and continuing to make clicking sounds and snapping my fingers.

The cat swishes its tail upward and looks like it's about to come to me when Mark pulls up.

"Come on." Stacey says.

It's not like I have a choice. If she goes, I follow.

"I had it this time. A minute longer, I would have had it. Damn."

She doesn't respond as she opens the passenger door of Mark's car and climbs in, giving a sheepish "hello."

I deposit myself in the backseat, per her wish, still lamenting my near-missed connection with the cat.

Mark and Stacey chat, gossiping about their mutual disdain for a coworker, while I stare out the window at buildings I can never visit because Staccy has little interest or need for them.

"It's funny how much you miss as you glide through life." I say, though Stacey ignores me. "Like, what's in that pawn shop? Who works at Baird's? There's always cars there, and I have no idea what's in there."

No response.

I look the other direction and see a series of willows. "That's where I died. Wait…where are we going?"

Stacey flinches and looks around herself. "I thought we were going to Morrison's?"

"I know this place out here that does karaoke that's a lot more fun." Mark promises. "Smaller, more audience participation; you've got such a great voice, you deserve a real audience."

"No…" Stacey says, though her voice sounds caught in her throat. "No, we can't go there."

Mark is already pulling into the bar. "What do you mean?

Stacey can't put the words together. Mark knows she's been to prison, but not that this was the bar.

He gets out of the car. Stacey doesn't, still trying to figure out how to tell the truth. Before he notices she's stalling, though, I hover my hand over her shoulder, unable to touch her. "You can't beat yourself up forever. You know I've forgiven you."

"I haven't forgiven myself." She says, her voice flat.

Its lack of emotion sends a shudder through me.

She puts a smile on as she gets out of the car. There's no outward protest, but I can tell she has decided to fake a good time.

Mark holds the door for her, but she sort of shuffles her way into the bar. I think at first out of reservation, though when she makes eye-contact with me and gives me a smile, I realize it was her way of *holding* the door for me. I would have passed through anyway, something she knows, but I appreciate her consideration. Maybe my reminder and Mark unwittingly forcing catharsis could be reaching her.

Stacey and Mark order sodas, and Stacey is kind enough to offer me a drink by placing a water in front of me at the chest high table we've occupied. There's a shift happening before my eyes. She and Mark laugh at, and with, bad singers, applaud decent ones, and cheer for the genuinely good.

"See, I told you you needed to get out." I say to her. I don't have to rise above the din, she can hear me no matter what.

"You were right!"

Mark looks at her. "What?" he shouts.

I laugh as she fumbles about, repeating herself.

But then she adds, "I haven't been here since the accident. This is the place I was leaving when I… I left this place too drunk to drive. I was 23; that's not an excuse, I know what I did was wrong. I sang, I think I didn't get the reaction I was looking for, and left in a huff. That's when I hit a car from behind at a stop sign and the driver died. When I hit a car and *killed* the driver. Lorelei."

She doesn't often say my name out loud. It's not unusual, friends and couples can go countless days without calling each other by name.

13

This is ownership, though. She's taking responsibility for the death she caused that night and recognizing who she killed.

Mark is patient and attentive. He doesn't take another drink while she's talking. He has zeroed in on her and he hears what she's saying. I like him.

"I had forgotten how fun this is." Stacey says, attempting to transition back to having the good time she was trying to avoid. "I guess I had forgotten how to have fun."

"Maybe you weren't letting yourself." Mark and I say at the same time.

I say "Jinx!"

Sadly, no one owes me a Coke.

My senses are becoming fuzzy, I feel like I'm drunk, and I think I know what's happening. "C'mon, Stacey…it's time!"

She looks at me strangely, maybe because I don't say her name out loud often, either. She follows me, though. Mark is left wondering what has dragged her away.

I point at the song book, miraculously open to the page that has the song I remember her singing that night. She gulps and looks at me, and I nod. She looks at Mark who gives her a thumbs-up, realizing what she's up to. And with that, she lets the D.J. know which song she'll sing.

The crowd cheers as the first notes sound. Stacey sings to the crowd, to Mark, and to me, the few quizzical looks from onlookers as she stares into empty space be damned. I sing with her, the crowd sings with her, and I can feel an effervescence beyond anything I felt in life.

With the song's end, the bar explodes in applause. The D.J. announces that he'll be taking a break because it would be hard to top an act like that. No one seems to mind as they cheer Stacey's performance. Mark pushes through to her to give her hearty congratulations, but he meets with her at the same time as a woman pushing as urgently to meet her and shoving a card into her hand.

"My name is Victoria, I produce some local bands and I would love to meet with you at my studio! That's impressive mastery over your vocals *and* the crowd."

I was excited for Stacey, and I could see she was ecstatic. Mark was floored, almost literally, tripping over himself in mutual excitement for the happenstance that a producer would be in the crowd. Somehow, though, I'm headed for the door.

Stacey wasn't following, but I was able to increase my distance from her. My tether now severed. As I exit the bar, I can feel the energy radiating from the place. Stacey knocked it out of the park, she shared a hard truth, she would be fine.

I can see the buildings and street, I see other people, though no one notices me. I'm on a new track, like following Stacey, only this is in a different direction. I found the stop sign where I died. Willow fronds threaten to cover it over.

"Someone should cut that back." I say to the empty intersection.

I wonder if that contributed to Stacey's accident.

"No." Her voice says behind me. "It was my fault. I shouldn't have been driving."

"You can read my thoughts now?"

She shrugs. "Maybe it's something I've tried to reason to myself before. Maybe it's always been excuses. Maybe you were my excuse to not forgive myself."

"Aha!" I laugh. "I told you ghosts aren't real!"

"Thank you." She says. "Whatever it is you are, thank you for sticking with me."

"I guess I'm being replaced by a sense of value and self-worth."

She smiles, but there's sadness to it.

"Don't go getting sentimental." I say. "What you did was wrong, don't you dare forget it—or me! But, be the best 'you' you can be moving forward. And you have my permission to be happy."

"Your *permission*?"

"Damn straight."

Mark catches up to her, their words sounding distant as I retreat from the street into the trees.

"What is it?" he asks. "You bolted out of there in a hurry, is everything okay?"

She turns to look, I know she does, but we don't see each other's faces.

15

Because I'm not there. Ghosts aren't real. There's nothing but the willows.

WARNING CRY

ATG

The first time it happened it went viral. Funny that… It indeed spread through the zeitgeist, but maybe it was that media saturation that caused the rest. *Hmm.* Anyway—yes, it went viral. How could it not? A woman mid-sentence on the nightly news screws up her face and lets out a blood curdling scream only to continue on as if nothing happened. It was on all the video sharing services, mixed into videos, spliced with scenes from horror movies to give her some reason to scream like she did. To her, though, there was no reason and she had no recollection it even occurred.

Lisa Browning had to be shown the recording to believe anything had happened. There was no look of dread, build up, or even a deep breath, just, "The collection will be on dis—" face and scream "—play through the end of the month."

She was the weekend anchor covering the weekly evening news for the first time, filling in for the vacationing regular. Some thought it was stress and anxiety. She was the topic of much debate and the public wanted to know more; or to see her scream again.

Her medical exams provided no insight. Psychiatric evaluations explained nothing either. No physical malady or mental condition could be found. She was perfectly healthy. Even undergoing hypnosis, despite being spoiled by seeing the event as the world saw it, she gave no indication that anything other than her reading from a teleprompter occurred. The scream, it seemed, would remain a mystery.

Unsurprisingly, though sadly, she lost her career and faded into internet obscurity. Until, of course, the rumors started to spread. Random people, with no real world connection to her whatsoever, were said to have issued the same dire expression and reaction to some unseen force, only to be completely unaware of having done so. The public at large thought it was a series of pranks, until it was caught on film again.

A group of friends in a basement parlor recorded their revelries. A young man playing pool contorted his face as though he saw something terrifying, let out a distressed cry, then proceeded to make a nice three rail bank shot. Everyone laughs, until he becomes visually upset and distressed that he's not in on whatever the joke is.

Those among the public stricken, once too embarrassed, trickled into emergency rooms with weird tales. Lisa was called back in, along with the billiard playing young man, to be examined extensively. Still yet, no indication of ailment.

The only thing remotely similar in medical history was *klazomania*, a condition of compulsive shouting, though that was closely associated with encephalitis and more persistent while the sufferer was aware of what they were doing. *The Scream*, as it came to be called, people only ever did it the one time. As cases grew in number, always the same thing, sometimes documented, mostly not, doctors and scientists had to wonder if there wasn't a mass hysteria occurring. There was a *dancing plague* in France, after all.

The urban legends cropped up; that anyone who did it would die so much time later. No one did. Air quality was blamed, but reports came from all around the world in very different climes. People were given a vision of some horrible thing as a warning to change their ways, Hell, demons, past sins, etc. Too many people of varying ages, reputes, and beliefs succumbed for that to hold water.

It went from interesting, to scary, to funny, to annoying, to nothing more exciting than a sneeze. You had your Scream and it was done with. No one ever remembered actually doing it so there was nothing to dread. It just happened. You might get lucky and be caught on video and pull an exceptional face that gets a lot of views on the Internet. The Scream had just become a rite of passage, though what it meant, no one knew. There were still some trying to study it, but for the most part, it was passé—until it was caught under the most fortuitous of conditions.

19

You see, I have multiple sclerosis. It's in remission and I feel fine, don't worry about me. I have to get MRIs every so often to check for lesions on my brain. My Scream came while I was having just such a test. I remember the lights dimming ever so slightly, like an air conditioner had kicked on, then a blink of darkness, and the staff asking after my well-being and generally freaking out.

The event had been recorded. The cocktail they load you with before going into the tube lit up in unexpected areas and ways. Somehow it affected the machinery as well, hence I saw the lights dim. My minor blackout was also different from others' experience and now doctors had concrete material to examine. As far as my MS, everything was fine. The data they had would take days, weeks, *years* to pore over. I was free to go.

There was a media sensation. I was contacted for interviews from every imaginable content provider. Even timid e-mails from tiny local papers in places I couldn't point to on a map. I would say the flash-in-the-pan fame was taste enough and when it died down I was happy to relax.

As my world shrunk back down I noticed myself become more anxious. Surely it was the whirlwind experience of free flights, hotels, dinners, and touring the television circuit. The jetlag of visiting far off countries for a few minutes on camera with people whose words I didn't understand were certainly stressful. It wasn't all media, either. Doctors the world over wanted to meet me as well. I was under a constant barrage of scrutiny. The first day I experienced complete silence from the outside world, I felt unperturbed. I could rest on my own time.

The nightmare I had upon my eyes sliding shut had me nearly vomiting as I screamed so hard in terror.

I was alone. No neighbors heard me. No significant other or pets to express concern. I was alone in facing a vision so terrible I was horrified at the idea of attempting to go back to sleep. As my head cleared I reasoned it was *only* a nightmare. Surely the fast-paced stresses I had faced the weeks prior had strained my mind.

At the time I only had the one dream. I could not shake the overwhelming dismay, however. It had been so vivid it stuck with me for days. Stress exacerbates MS. Maybe I had pushed too hard for too long. I was in regular contact with my doctor anyway, especially with any new details about what they had found in my MRI. She agreed I might be reacting to nervous tension and invited me in for a once over.

"So, I'm just curious," she said after pleasantries, "what was the dream?"

I felt my hands go cold and tingly. "Just thinking about it sets me on edge…and it's all I can think about. I don't really want to talk about it."

I said it looking at my knees. There was something in my face, though, with the way she looked at me when I finally made eye contact. She gave the briefest of nods as though somehow I had frightened her and she couldn't wait to get out of the room.

The uncomfortable silence stretched as she did her cursory examination of my vitals. I complied with her quiet monosyllabic requests. When she was done she started typing into her phone, a prescription that would print out at the desk.

"It probably is stress." She droned. "Your heartbeat is strong, but elevated. I'm going to give you some serotonin for anxiety and something to help you sleep. We'll see where you are in two months on how to go forward."

"What—" I scowled and shook my head. "What do you *know*?"

She stared at me and chewed the inside of her bottom lip. "Your brain lit up like you were having a full sensory experience; sight, sound, scent… Areas of your amygdale associated with processing *fear* reacted severely."

"So my brain experienced something like I was actually there…wherever *there* is…for just a moment. A hallucination?"

"The areas of your brain responsible for memory formation also activated. I can't tell you what any of this means; they're still looking it over. We just saw parts of your brain light up in a concert of recognizable features. All of it together is similar to tests we perform while in the MRI specifically to see these things happen. As far as that half-second, your brain was under the impression something terrifying happened to your entire being…and you may have a memory of it.

21

"It wasn't just your brain, though. There's constant diagnostics on the machine as well. Engineers and technicians think they recorded what actually caused your Scream, but not necessarily the *how*. They think they might be able to replicate it, make it happen on purpose."

I could feel the twisting in my gut forming a Gordian Knot. "So your apprehension is that my nightmare was actually that memory. They're going to ask me to go in again to see if they can cause a Scream."

Looking at her, the disturbed expression that flashed upon her face before she turned away, I realized what my own must have looked like. "They're sure they can do it and they think they can hold that, *moment*, open; am I right?"

"I didn't think anything of it until I saw how frightened you were. You don't have to do anything you don't want to."

"I know." I nodded. "But it's not really about me at this point is it? If we can find out what's causing this, what it means, I kind of have a duty; don't I?"

She didn't answer, not even with body language. Part of me wished she would. Part of me wanted to run screaming from the office and run for the hills. If my nightmare was a memory…I dare not say it. The thought of taking my own life to avoid something is anathema to me. Nevertheless, the thought occurred.

In the subsequent week, sleep was sparse and fleeting. Dreams were normal, but the memory of the nightmare, that might itself be a memory, continued to haunt my waking hours. Bright sunny days were no bastion. Shadows of even simple things—*fence posts*—held horrors that were sure to jump me if I looked away. A closed door hid things that would flay me alive. Worse yet, open, *darkened* doors beckoned me, tempted me to accept oblivion and fall into their yawning abyss.

The doctor's prescriptions were of little help. I was an anxious mess come testing day. I had resolved to participate, however, so I arrived on time to get to the bottom of humanity's plague of screams. Perhaps, even resolve and end my nightmare vision.

The MRI technicians were sure they could reproduce the power surge that accompanied my Scream. All of this in hopes of recreating the event. If it worked, I would be the first person to experience the enigma twice. If in experiencing it a second time I could help reveal to the world what had afflicted us, surely I could muster the courage to face a fright. It was just a vision. So I told myself. If what I was about to see for a protracted amount of time to gather information was *half* as scary as my nightmare threatened to be…I must continue to rebuke the thought.

The contrast medium injected before my scan is warm. I can feel it spread throughout my body. It's not painful, but unnerving; this is not a sensation you typically feel. The human body knows when something is out of the ordinary and the fight or flight response is quick to respond. The process might be safe, I've even gotten used to it, but every time there's an urge to tear away and run as far as I can.

This time, I'm only given noise-canceling headphones, no music. They want my full attention focused on the experiment. Going into the tube is ominous, the sounds of electric motors moving the table sound distant and muffled. There's a murmur of voices and I call out "what," realizing I shouted far too loud.

A voice buzzes through the headphones, "Sorry, I didn't open the channel. There's a panic button off the right side of the table. As much as we want you to try and endure for the duration of the scan, if it becomes too much, press it and we'll stop."

I attempt to respond quieter this time, focusing on the feeling of my voice within my chest. The "thanks" probably still comes out too loud.

I feel the vibrations of the drumbeat coming from the MRI more than I hear them. The curious effect causes me to focus, everything is so far away. I'm in a quiet space with only the sound of my own breathing and rooms, or *miles*, away there is a dull *thump-thump-thump*.

After several minutes of relative silence I realize just how terribly boring this could end up being. Focusing on my breathing, I give meditation a shot. Hopefully I can calm myself and make it through the test without going mad.

When I think I hear the murmurs of voices again, I call out (again too loudly) reminding them I can't hear them talking. There's no response. Not even in the negative that no one had been talking. Just the varying tones in vibration and thuds surround me.

"I think there's something wrong with the headphones."

No response.

"Hello?"

Nothing.

Barely able to move my head in any direction, I strain to look down toward my feet. There's no activity and still only the sound of the machine. Moving my right hand toward the panic button, I notice that I can see swirling stars in my eyes. I've seen this before, under duress. Stand up too fast or hit your head and the eyes are robbed of blood flow, causing an error in your vision. I only know this because I've seen it so many times. Maybe I've lain here too long, maybe I'm just stressing myself out. Maybe I was actually asleep and didn't call out at all.

"Hell—"

There's a *whooshing* sound inside my whole body and the lights dim like they did before, but don't brighten back up.

"—o?"

The machine sounds are even further away, but the stars are brighter. It occurs to me they're no longer swirling. I'm looking at an actual field of stars.

The air around me feels frigid, though the light of the stars is hot. It's a still day, standing in snow while feeling the warmth of the sun, only a million times over. Afraid I'm full-on hallucinating, the urge to press the button is even stronger. I just want to keep my finger on it. When I reach, though, it's not there. Nor is the bed, the head restraint, the machine…or even my body.

I can feel myself move, or, at least I think I can. When I look down there is nothing, I do not see myself, only an endless space full of dazzling white stars. I wave my hands in front of my face, they are free, but not there. I only see the stars.

Calling out again, my voice is this time unrestrained, though my words are unclear. More, guttural sounds. The stars move, vertigo rushes through me. Weightlessness and lack of a body make it difficult to regain my bearings. It was small at first, just a waver that made me feel unbalanced. Perhaps it was I who moved? No. The stars brighten as if in response to my turmoil. So bright I want to shield my eyes, yet, I have no hands, no *eyelids* to squint. I am bathed in such dazzling brightness that I can feel the intensity of it in the back of my brain…if it's even here.

The stars move again, their white light burning so bright it changes into colors I cannot even comprehend. These are colors not meant for the human eye. These are ultraviolet, infrared, x-ray, microwave, things beyond even the realm of science, yet I can see them all. The stars swinging along on their blanket of darkness, now filled with a swirling medium that makes me ill to see, for seeing it is the same as feeling an unknown agent against my skin.

Apprehension fills me as recognition gives way to dread. The blanket and its stars are the shell of a thing that is turning to gaze upon me. This is a thing that should not, *cannot*, be seen, though this is the second time I have witnessed its existence. My nightmare is made clear before me. There is no analogue to this…*thing*. It is filled with intelligence and malice and hunger. Where it feeds there is nothing but agony and horror overflowing with the eternal screams of things that do not understand. It is wider than the whole of the universe. Its appetite is its reason for being. The insatiable *craving* that drives this chaos made of stars and death is the desire to destroy creation.

I can see the thing Lisa Browning saw and in her seeing showed us all. This is the face of God, of all the gods, of every demon we dared imagine. All of our fears are nothing compared to it.

The Scream rises where my throat should be, but I make no sound. It sees me. Whatever sensory organs it has, if it even has things we can compare to anatomy, it sees me and desires.

Far away, as if voices desperately called through the winds of a storm, I can hear people cry "what do you see" and "are you all right" and "can you hear me?" The monstrosity can hear them. Or taste them? I do not know.

If it has tentacles, they move like bolts of lightning. If there are claws, they scrape at the very fabric of space like nails on a chalkboard. Where a body should be I cannot tell, but there is the open maw of a shooting victim's gaping, bleeding wounds. I am horrified and disgusted, fearful for my life and all of reality, yet, struck with indefinable awe. Is it beautiful? Is a being of pure terror and destruction also something to be marveled?

The voices come again, closer. If I had an ear they would be shouting directly onto my eardrum. "Please tell us you are all right!"

A creature larger than all of the cosmos closes on me and these pithy humans worry after *my* well being? I have no way to express to them the urgency of the message I have become witness to. If it has senses, a concept I realize is far too limited for what I see, it focuses them on me and those behind me that try to gain my attention.

It does not speak, but the message is clear. We are but sugar trapped in the vessels of a fruit rotting on a vine we cannot see. My awareness shifts beyond this devourer of heavenly plains. It is a mere insect. The *truth* is beyond it, for even it does not know the more gruesome levels of destruction and chaos that loom over it. And beyond that. And beyond that.

I can see the entire chain.

"What do you see?" the voices call out again.

So I say, "Everything."

My voice is alien and wrong. It is too small and weak to convey my intent. I will spend the rest of my life trying to describe my experience and I will not have succeeded in describing one micron. The voice is so feeble I am denied the privilege of my audience with this living eternity and am slammed back into my sack of flesh.

I am disappointed, but there is comfort in this. Life will expire. Be it by my hands or at the hands of time, my existence will end and I will be spared the horror of the truth I have seen. Our stars, our galaxies, our *universe*, are nothing more than moss upon the back of a bug laying waste to crops. A bug who is the prey of another bug, who is the plaything to a cat, who is the antagonist to a dog that yields to a farmer that cultivates the fields and decides what measures are best suited to deal with the parasites that plague his land. And so on above him. And above him. And above him.

As the muted whir of electric motors crank the table out of the MRI machine, I see the fluorescent bulbs for the paltry farce of what light is.

There is a recognizable horror, disappointment, and relief in the technician's eyes. He saw it, too. I do not even need to speak.

"Many did." He whispers in the affirmative.

Like metronomes falling in and out of sync, hundreds of millions saw at the same time I did. Some understood and found life wanting. Others went mad before they could realize the scope. The message had been made clear and life would go on regardless, feeding on itself as it does.

What started as a scream, a funny thing on the internet that everyone saw, led to everyone seeing so much more. Our minds had been too weak to even retain the vision. We could only scream in the moment the truth reached us then forget as our bodies desperately tried to protect us.

But now that we know what is coming, everyone is screaming.

DEPTH
ST

//Begin Transcriptionist's Log of Lt. Harper Santoro. Communications Oversight and Operations aboard the I.S.O. Border Patrol Ship IND4736, regarding the cosmic event that destroyed both ship and crew.

Transcription follows://

Captain Maryam Jibril has ordered us to write our last testimonies.

If we're not already dead.

I'm writing, though.

Barely anything works. Red light and screaming sirens. A tinny recording of the ship's doctor plays on repeat through hardware emergency speakers that usually only beep indicating an error. It's the only way he can reach as many of us as possible with the ship's systems all failing.

We were exposed to a massive amount of radiation from an unknown source. It flashed us with no warning. The doctor must have awoken before I did and prepared those of us who would be unfortunate enough to continue waking up. Our emergency distress beacon is hard shielded against such events and has been activated, but everything on a computer is dead and gone, just like us.

Hence writing.

Lt. Bradley had alerted me to a strange signal before we blacked out. Ship to ship? Command to ship? There was syntax, form, but— indecipherable. A strange sound, like birdsong, or a parrot mimicking Russian.

Bradley must be dead.

The ping was from somewhere else. It wasn't from the known lanes of radio traffic. A Russian ship scanning us? Was it a code we had intercepted? Our readings had come almost simultaneously with the radiation burst.

The broadcast and sirens halted.

Dr. Nanjiani has interrupted his own recording, his voice is small and crackling. He tells us the emergency beacon should have been received by now, so even if it fails, we are not forgotten. He then proceeded to tell us how the ship, and us, will die.

Basically: we melt from the inside or suffocate, but one will happen regardless. He said it much nicer. He is a good doctor.

He mirrors the Captain's orders, advocating for written documentation of everything we can think of.

I'm writing a letter to the future.

So are a few others around me.

But the birdsong—what was that?

We're being cooked alive.

We had been scanned, or were being scanned—was the scan the source of the radiation? Russian birdsong weapon?

//Begin Transcriptionist's Notation: A smear has blocked the passage written here. Depth analysis of indentations indicate the word "Context" written a few times in a row.

End Transcriptionist's Notation.//

A new kind of weapon for space warfare? Something so strong it could penetrate redundant shielding and turn our boat into a microwave oven?

Would there ever be a way to tell from where someone had fired something like that?

But the signal from somewhere else seemed like a probe, radar, an information searching signal, not destructive. Why the strange, coded language along with it? Buried within it? Every ship pings their respective Command. Codes aren't unusual, but unless you know what you're listening for and where to listen for it, there's slim chance you'd ever intercept an important message. Conversely, signal trash gets picked up all the time.

Right before we blacked out, I was looking at other channels, and the birdsong seemed to echo throughout the channels. Louder on some, trickling static but recognizable within others.

My family knows I love them. We had a tearful goodbye when I went away. However, any time someone ships out, there's always the chance... I had thought about my sister and when she left on her tour. Everyone entertains dark fantasies of losing a loved one that comes with the anxiety of possibly losing a loved one, right? They would understand if I didn't leave any personal notes.

I love you, mom, dad, and Charlize.

That'll be enough.

Sometimes stars make signals we can hear, the Cosmic Microwave Background is a constant static on all channels, and Fast Radio Bursts make eerie sounds, but this was regular, coded, a broadcast. Not just noise.

I think of the poor people at Vesuvius, forever remembered as crude concrete corruptions mistaken for ash. Our mysterious dead bodies would be all we were remembered for. We will be a ghost ship.

Wait.

Bradley said something was outside the ship. He said the name of what was outside the ship. Then there was the proximity alert, sudden, instantaneous. Then we blacked out. Our terminals were dead, whatever he had read in that moment was gone forever and he's not writing anything.

Didn't it start with a K?

//Begin Transcriptionist's Notation: Another dark smear obscures this passage; however it is legible, "Ghost ship? K? Kojin-maru. A Japanese mining freighter. A lost vessel, a ghost story the mining community shares, supposedly seen at random, always way outside of shipping lanes."

End Transcriptionist's Notation.//

A few accidents have happened, and those vessels had been found off shipping lanes in predictable arcs. The Kojin-maru was gone. Nothing. Vanished.

Bradley had identified the Kojin-maru before we blacked out. The birdsong became clearest right before.

Connected?

I need to get to a porthole. I would normally ask the captain permission, but she looks dead.

I must manually open a few doors—I hope I can continue writing in a moment.

//Begin Transcriptionist's Notation: Writing becomes fainter here, depth analysis helped fill in the majority of the remaining.
End Transcriptionist's Notation.//

Found porthole, a window in the floor.

Ultraviolet, a blacklight in space, incredibly dark yet unbearably bright. An intense purple mass—or pink? —and struck through like kintsugi with lines of black and gold.

I am waiting until our ship's rotation will bring me back around to see it again. I think I know what to look for.

It is the Kojin-maru. Affected—infected—by some transfiguration that has set the ship ablaze with strange energy. I have no other words for it. It's pink, purple, yet marbleized with veins of something black and gold. It is glowing in ultraviolet, and I am certain by how it looks—that it is suddenly here—it must be the source of the radiation.

I kept watch, but it did not come into view a third time, nor after several revolutions. It was there, and then it wasn't.

//Begin Transcriptionist's Notation: There is a light sketch of the ship Santoro describes, which appears to match known schematics of the Kojin-maru at the time of its disappearance.
End Transcriptionist's Notation.//

I returned to my station out of habit. I saw Bradley's notebook open. One note is written.

"Kojin-maru. Space shook. Every signal bent to Kojin's position—light. Something buried."

//Begin Transcriptionist's Notation: Cross-reference verified.
End Transcriptionist's Notation.//

If the Kojin-maru's appearance attracted every known wavelength, from radio to light, like a primordial blackhole, then listening for the birdsong on its strongest channel in the moment the Kojin appeared should give the clearest signal. Data recorders from around this sector—if they've survived—should have every signal from in- and outbound communications, surveillance, and general observations. A focal point twisting those communications, though, it might be hard to parse the layers of information.

Shit.

If space warped around the Kojin in the moment it appeared, then the data would be compressed into a single signal. It would be hard to decode, but the information would be there. Sound and light, fused. Untangling it all will be a nightmare.

I'm sorry to whomever gets assigned that task.

New technologies will be developed to peel apart the layers, but woe is the poor intern who will have to read countless transcripts over and over again.

The birdsong is between bands—likely interstellar. Not known code. Only heard it as a precursor to Kojin-maru's appearance. Visual confirmation of Kojin's presence and disappearance. Listen beyond solar system. Kojin-maru's place attracts signal. Scanning? Something is looking for the Kojin-maru, but the Kojin-maru found us. Something is in deep space. Something is coming.

Looking at us and finding us as we die due to a bizarre natural disaster.

Confirmation of intelligent life. Seeing a ghost ship. Dying of radiation poisoning. Becoming the next ghost ship. All on the same day. Could be worse.

I love you, mom, dad, and Charlize.

//End Transcription//

CAMPING
THW

The last time I went camping, I was only fourteen years old. I had gone with my mother and her boyfriend and was allowed to invite my best friend. I remember it fondly—mostly. As fondly as the memory of sleeping on lumpy ground in summer can really be.

We took a long weekend. But instead of feeling like my internal clock had been reset by the natural day/night cycle, I was exhausted for that first week back home. Not just because of a lot of play and adventure. We had seen bison. It was the first time I had seen a scorpion in the wild. I had my first taste of dark lager, and it was gross. It wasn't even the lack of creature comforts, like a bed or air-conditioning, but because of a terror that kept me awake after the first night.

That first night, I fell asleep fine but was awoken in the middle of the night by hushed voices and wavering lights. People were milling about the campsite in the middle of the night. I thought it was strange, probably kids, maybe even *adults*, fooling around. I turned my head away from the edge of the tent to avert my eyes from brief flashes of light filtering through the canvas. As it turned out, turning my head may have saved my life.

The next morning, my friend and I were regaled by other campers of a bison having crossed straight through the campsite in the night. The people that had been up with their flashlights had been trying to usher the beast through the camp without trampling anyone's tent. As we mused at how close we were to wildlife, I remembered something else from my midnight disturbance: heavy breathing.

No one had actually followed the tracks through the entire campsite yet. In fact, it had lumbered straight through *our* site. That sound of breathing compelled me to carefully step alongside the cloven imprints, closer to mine and my friend's tent, closer to *my* side of the tent, until I saw the mud actually *on* our tent. Lifting the canvas from the ground showed the depression in the earth of where the behemoth had stepped directly on the tent. I slipped inside to see the corresponding impression from within. It was mere inches from my pillow. Had I not rolled over, it very well could have put all of its easily one thousand pounds directly onto my forehead. I was excited and horrified all at once.

Sharing the tale in my best spooky tones with my twelve-year-old son from across a campfire, however, left him unimpressed. I think he hoped I had been stepped on so I could show off a gnarly scar as a trophy. Still, it was a good opportunity to remind him not to be loud and obnoxious or to overreact to strange situations.

This trip, another long weekend like so long ago, was his idea. He wanted to go camping and I wasn't about to discourage a sense of adventure. It would be just the two of us, a "guy's weekend." Maybe he would love it and it could become a hobby for us. Maybe he would hate it and we'd never have to do it again. Considering that, I borrowed some gear from a friend and we were off.

Much like my last trip, we spent the first day adventuring. We set up our spot, well away from any other campers this time, the park not being very full. We hiked and saw birds not found in neighborhoods, furry critters from a distance and even eating from our hands, and we were even taken by surprise as we stood at the edge of a stream when a deer came to drink less than ten feet away without giving us a second glance. We wound down our hike laughing about the choice of phrasing on a trail's notice board: "Please do not molest the plants and wildlife."

We stayed up late. Talked video games, movies, and how gross the human body is. Also, how gross beer is (he only had a small sip). The fire died down to occasional soft blue wisps darting up out of glowing coals. Above us, a sea of stars unlike anything he'd ever seen. I felt a little guilty about not having done this sooner, more often, but glad we had this time together now.

When he inevitably started to fall asleep in his reclined lawn chair, I nudged him awake. "Why don't we go ahead and call it a night, hunh?"

He nodded, offering no fight. He lurched up and toward the tent like a zombie. I chuckled and promised I'd be right in. "I just need to douse the fire."

However, I took my time. Waiting to hear his movements come to a stop, I fished around in my backpack and pulled out a joint to enjoy on my own. The hum of crickets and frogs provided the perfect white noise to zone out to. I stared at the smear of blue and white that comprised the Milky Way, thinking maybe a regular camping expedition wouldn't be so terrible.

Relaxing contemplation was interrupted by a distinct crack of wood. Adrenaline surged, but my physical response was delayed. I looked behind me, seeing upside down trees as I craned my neck backwards from my own reclined chair. Nothing was there, save a dim, yellow streetlight on the road several yards away. Something moved, I could hear it, but the only movement to see was bugs around the light.

I sat up to properly look over my shoulder. Black silhouettes of still trees were framed against the starry sky and solitary electric light. My brain felt wrapped in gauze as I fought to see through a haze that dulled the fear I knew I should feel, knew I *would* feel in just a moment, absolutely positive I would erupt in an impulse to run, laugh, hide, and cover my mouth to not wake my son, because I knew, just *knew*, it was a raccoon or a deer or something…

I shook my head.

Nothing there.

"You are way too high." I whispered to myself.

Pulling out a small LED flashlight from my pack, I shined it through the trees. Crickets noticeably silenced themselves, but it wasn't a complete silence. Something was moving. There was a shifting of grass, irregular, but certainly moving.

"It has to be something small that I'm not thinking to look for."

I heard my son shift in his sleeping bag. I made a shushing sign with my finger against my lips. Not to him, but to myself, *I must remember to keep my thoughts internal!*

Slowly sweeping the light around me, I shifted on the chair, creaking and making my own obnoxious noises to further disrupt the sounds of nature. The disturbance of grass and leaves seemed to grow closer. Before I could turn fully around, I saw it in my periphery.

It spooked me at first. I thought for sure a deer had wandered up next to me, probably curious about our campsite and the dying fire, docile like the deer at the creek. I slowed my motions even more, feeling giddy about this new brush with nature. The pale white I saw from the corner of my eye was not the white fur of a deer's breast, however.

My light found a leg, matted fur or hair appeared to be caked with mud and ended with a cloven hoof in the ground. It trembled slightly, quavering to hold the weight above. The angle was wrong, though, it bent backward like a hind leg, but no four-legged creature stood before me. The dull, dirty fur gave way in patches to sickly gray skin. It was taught, stretched too far, nearly to ripping at the joint. The skin was bruised and may have bled already. I didn't move the light any further, but my gaze continued up along something resembling a human thigh, again, elongated and stretched too far.

I felt sick. Whatever buzz I had vanished and I may have cursed. I couldn't be certain; fear had replaced high, and a part of me was resisting accepting what stood before me. I could feel the heat coming off of it. I could hear it *breathing.*

My son shifted in the tent again. "Dad?" he called tiredly.

The thing next to me shifted at the sound.

"*Shh,*" I sounded. "Stay quiet, son, there's a—"

What was this thing? I couldn't tear my eyes away, but nothing about it made sense. I didn't want to turn my attention away, but tried to keep my voice measured for my son.

"There's a deer," I whispered. "Very close to the tent. Just stay quiet, don't spook it."

"Seriously? Can I see?" his voice sounded more awake now, excited.

37

"No, stay still… Stay *quiet*."

He harrumphed. Meanwhile, I could feel myself quivering, fearful for our lives.

It looked like a mockery of a man, broken into awkward angles, its skin stretched over bones too long. It had weeping wounds at joints. Bone poked through the ends of its fingers forming ragged claws. The fingers twitched with pain and agitation. As I looked higher and higher up along its frame, I could see the entire thing was stretched too far. It labored just to keep itself upright. Its midsection concave, its very organs protruded from underneath the bruised skin and made a lumpy pot belly over exposed male genitalia. I could see that, even as it hunched over, it rose at least ten feet high.

The chest expanded slowly, shakily, lifting shoulders and arms with each breath. There was no vocalization, but the breath raked through a raw sounding throat behind a hanging jaw.

Cracked and rotting teeth glistened with saliva and blood. Its tongue lolled, restless and fidgeting. Glassy eyes darted back and forth, not settling on anything. Its face contorted; though, if it was sensing anything, I couldn't tell. Part of me hoped it was blind, whatever *it* was.

My hand shifted, shaking the flashlight, and the thing finally reacted to my presence. It rolled its head to face me, shifting slightly to accommodate the weight of a massive rack of antlers. They looked black against the trees and sky above. Its eyes stopped and focused directly on me and my flashlight. Mouth still agape, it sniffed and took in its surroundings, regarding the still glowing coals in the fire pit and the tent next to me.

Never making a sound beyond sniffs and breath, it slowly raised one hand toward my head. Every fiber of muscle tensed and prepared me to attempt to get away, but the hand did not reach me. Instead, it raised its broken and bloody claws to its neck and scratched lightly. Despite its delicate movement, welts formed on the skin there in reaction to the exposed boney digits.

The heavy breath grew deeper into a sigh as it walked away from me, nearly dragging its hooves. It avoided the fire pit, but walked straight through our site and into the trees opposite from me.

Thinking, perhaps too late, I should try to document this sight, I grabbed my phone out of my pack and opened the camera, just pressing my finger against the shutter button to engage the burst-shot mode. It stopped just a moment and looked to its right, but continued to ignore me, and then left, disappearing into the darkness beyond my flashlight's reach.

I sat what felt like a good long while until I felt like I was "safe."

"Dad?"

I nearly fell off my chair.

My son was peeking through the tent flap. "What was it?"

"Uh…"

I looked back down at my phone and began flipping through blurry, poorly shot pictures. *Typical*, I thought. In the middle of them, though, was one that looked like a deer's hindquarters in retreat. I showed him, and his lack of better knowledge convinced him I had managed to at least get a picture of an intruding deer fleeing.

"I wish I could have seen it," he groaned.

He sounded somewhat disappointed, yet still awestruck something had been so close. I shuttered as echoes of adults regaled kids of wildlife intruders.

"Maybe next time, son." I choked through a dry mouth. "Let's get to bed."

A SONG
ATG

The siren blares her breathless cacophony and we all march out to the beat of the shadow. Light, dark, light, dark; stop, move, stop, move. The blazing strobe a facsimile of her heartbeat. Light burning us to ash, dark giving up advance. There is nothing but this. There is an army of us versus the only one of her kind. Whispers in the dark claim there were others, but they were lost, burned out by their own songs.

We have always been, huddled until the song begins, marching when the light turns away and we can ascend. In quiet darkness, we sleep, dreaming things unsaid. Whispers from within our piled masses rise up, infecting dreams with purpose. They tell us, *warn* us, that to dream too loudly awakens the siren, but who can control what thoughts fill a dream?

The siren will sing regardless, those of us unmoored to the mound argue, "To sleep is to dream, and to dream is to sing a song, and that song will lift us high."

"And to fly is to die, for you will be dust upon her breath." The whispers counter.

The argument is moot, for we dream and she sings. That is the way.

Standing atop a mountain full of crags and pitfalls, it is only her, the song, and the pulsating light. She is an earthquake forever shaping a landscape we *must* navigate to reach her at the summit. Some are lost to the lure of shadows, seeking to escape the light, to just sit still until the song comes to an end. Some fall to darker things that lurk in the shadows, torn apart in deaths we cannot see or fathom. But there are those of us steadfast in our mission to reach the siren, some lost to the light, some finding our way.

The light is most intense at the provenance of her earthen platform, the shadow does not pulse here. We are ash and dust in a maelstrom, each concentrating to reach the pedestal at her feet. She does not see us, nor the dust or light. She sees nothing of her surroundings. There is only a song in one long note that beckons us all, forces us to move, even those that refuse. In choosing to hide, they are still answering the call. A single speck of ash smearing across the blank page at her feet and we are released, our effort rewarded with freedom—but freedom is not above. Those who make inscriptions will find themselves deeper in the mass, some so deep no light reaches them, no song calls them, they can only whisper.

We make single marks, some merely dots, some whole brush strokes. Eventually forming words in a language we know, but none of us can read. We give our single contribution and no more and are given no context to what we create. Sometimes whole pages of text flutter up and away from the pages of the book we write but cannot read. Once filled, they are ripped asunder and thrown up into the storm. In other times, only a single word is formed and the siren falls silent.

We care not. We must answer the call.

The few who can remember the last time the siren called, it was short, a moment really. Some clambered toward inevitability only to find most of us barely broke from the horde. Today, it is many. We are a deluge. We see page after unreadable page ascend and think, "Surely that is enough?" Yet, the song continues.

She is crying, the song hitched and staccato; is it coming to an end or only about to grow stronger?

The pulse of the shadow quickens, many of us reach the summit, even the cowards crawl cautiously forward. Is this a song worth hearing? Is this the song we may sing along with? Innumerable slashes and strokes form a text and fill a book we don't understand. In another place we will never see, a binding collects our efforts. The deepest whispers, somehow still reaching us even as we fulfill our duty, claim the book brings madness, that we are party to the end of another world.

Then the cry, her song, comes to an end. It is not the most strenuous effort we've been exposed to. But it carries portent. Something is coming. Something from above is poking at the siren, invoking her song, to call forth the horde and make the words.

When she sings, we will come. When the song is written, we will rest. And the whispers? They tell us not to dream, but they were dreamers once, and many.

SOMETHING IN THE WAY

THW

The line was longer on Fridays. The Salvation Army served a chowder with some honest to goodness protein that one day of the week. A few of the men from the Jungles—the Hooverville that had settled on the Seattle docks—would sneak up to get a bowl. Publicly, they despised the organized charity, the food didn't nourish, and their housing was worse than what a few men could put together from scraps. Sometimes the hunger got to them, though, and they would swallow their pride along with the gruel.

"How comes you only come up on Friday?" the—kid?—in front of me asks.

He's short, but so am I, and we're all very tired and hungry. He could be a stunted 18-year-old; he could be a broken 27. We all look the same anymore.

"Fish." I answer. "The Catholics serve fish on Friday. It's the only meat they actually put in their soups. It's the only meat they can get around here kinda cheap."

"Sometimes I find beef…" he shrugs.

I look at him questioning if he's sure about that.

He shrugs again.

"When I was a kid a tick bit me and I haven't been able to eat beef since." I tell him. He doesn't understand. "Their chicken soup is saltier than the sea, I think it made me sick when I tried it. But, fish—"

The shorter man interrupts, "Fish ain't got no feelings, so it's okay to eat 'em, right?"

"I think I've heard that." I say and shuffle forward with him a little.

"You ever worry about Jackson catching any of us accepting handouts?"

I didn't answer his question. Instead, I left the line.

Can't trust anyone. Won't trust anyone. I already said too much just being cordial.

There are cooks down in the Jungles, but it isn't always fish on the menu. They catch whatever they can corner, and docks tend to have rats. Cats chase rats. Dogs chase cats. Sometimes people fish on the docks, but dock-water fish has a—taste.

Eating is gambling, and everyone is cheating.

Nothing is fair. That's why we're here. Hundreds of us unemployed, unprotected by the state of Washington, by our government, left out to die in the cold because our employers couldn't count high enough to pay themselves. They've tried to burn us out, but we rebuild.

We have a "president," Jesse Jackson, who agreed with the city council that we would at least keep things civil on the docks. No women, no children. Easy enough. We could keep our own peace better than angry police.

When you're living under bridges, propping up boxes for walls and tarps for ceilings, life is only survival. So, what of it if I was in the line for a chunk of fish in cornmeal? Some kid gonna tell on me, make me feel worse so he can—I don't even know. Feel like he has power for a few seconds as someone yells at me?

Where I have settled, my neighbors don't much look in on me. I've found a nice corner to be quiet in, and it's there I retreat from the possible rat. The human one. There are indeed rodents running between our "houses" and people do catch them. Though I suspect more of them are kept as pets as are thrown into pots of boiling water.

Lighting my two candles before sunset, no one suspects anything. I pray to myself, covering my face with my hands. No one recognizes a ceremony or ritual, if they've seen anything, it's a man on his knees holding his face.

Who isn't sobbing into their hands for God's blessings these days?

It's when I complete the procedure, looking upon the lit candles for the beginning of the Sabbath, that I see her eyes. A—woman?—is sitting on the other side of my table looking at the candles and me, alternately. Something in those eyes makes me question if I'm even with a human. They seem too big, and they reflect too much light.

I inhale. At first in a gasp, but then to dredge up some words of accusation or curiosity. But my mind is reeling.

She says, "I like your light."

She blows them out in my face. In the rush of warm air from the candles, there is also a salty, cool air swirling through it. The sudden darkness blinds me to her movements, but I can hear her slip past me toward the door. I see her exit, turning the wrong direction to get anywhere, as I am against the wall, but she doesn't correct her course, she doesn't slip passed back by the doorway.

Following, worried about an intruder in the community, but also about a woman getting lost in the Jungles, I do not see her there against the retainer wall. From the other direction—the way in—a man's voice.

"You interested?"

"I'm afraid you have me at a loss, sir." I confess. "I'm not terribly fond of someone just coming into my house nor any insinuation that I may be *interested* in further invasion of my privacy."

He looks insulted and confused. I spoke too fast.

I step closer to him. "Look, women aren't allowed down here, you know that. You can't be endangering a lady like that. And lastly, no, I am not interested in anything you have on offer, take her over to Qwest Park, get someone who has a dollar. Just—leave me be."

"Hey, friend," he croons. "What's wrong with a little fish on Friday, am'I'right?"

"What?" I ask, narrowing my gaze at him.

Is this the kid's doing? Shouldn't have said anything.

Then the woman walks between us, as if she was standing there the entire time, though I did not see her. She moves strangely, *incorrectly*. It's not walking, or a dramatic sway of feminine hips. It's some sort of a pantomime of both. Something animating stilts with controls it's unfamiliar with.

She hangs on his shoulder with her hands. They are pale to the point of translucence. The knuckles seem particularly knobby. And she does sort of hang-on to him, those legs struggling to stand, to do what a normal person's legs are meant to do.

"I like his light." She says into his ear.

He smiles.

"It's okay to eat fish…" he says but doesn't complete the phrase.

Will she murder me? Will her man while she sucks my—

"No." I say as politely as I can muster despite the anxiety rising along my spine. "No, thank you."

He shrugs and doesn't say anything more.

"Good night, then." I say and retreat into my shack, closing my door (by placing a board I keep next to it over the entry).

In total darkness again, I wait to hear them shuffle away before stepping back from my "door." Voices mumble from another shack. A deal being made. I don't need to see anything. There's so little privacy between us and the world, I don't need to look. These men feel like they have needs, I can't blame them how they satisfy themselves. That's their lives.

When a man's scream wakes me from sleep, I do not leap to find the meaning. A lot of men scream. Nightmares, frustration, fights break out… But this scream was along the nightmare vein. Someone feeling like they're being dragged off, crushed, chased, murdered, covered in whatever they fear the most. Except, I'm awake enough to hear the scream stifled.

I'm awake enough to hear the movement of bodies against cloth, wood, and dirt. We *can* be protective of each other. Someone might yell "murder" to draw attention to a serious situation. But no one does.

Striking the match sounds like a powder keg explosion in the surrounding silence. I light one of my Shabbat candles, thankfully still alone in my own space. But the sounds continue outside without the interruption of others. Was I the only one to hear it?

Going out to investigate is both dangerous, as I have no weapons to defend myself, and the responsible thing to do, to protect my brothers in poverty. Trust no one, but I can't just *let* someone die. I

47

move my door and step into the alley with my candle, alerting absolutely no one. Nobody outside, and no other lights have been lit.

There is only the sound of surf several yards away.

Then the attempted sexy strut walks between shacks, her hands lightly touching her surroundings to maintain balance. My candlelight flickers back at me in the depths of those too large sockets. She sees me, her face distorts in the shadows, maybe into a smile. Otherwise, she makes no acknowledgment. She begins humming, but I can only hear the sound of it, not the tune. She disappears again between panels of darkness.

I curse myself, knowing I should try to go back to sleep. She makes me uncomfortable. Her man made me uncomfortable.

I find myself in the alleyway. A snore here, a shifting there, the distant surf, and a distinct dragging of something heavy against the earth. I rely on those sounds to follow them, knowing my candle would give me away, even if she did like it and hadn't told on me, yet.

Weaving through a block of shacks, we hit open sand. I have no choice when the wind takes out my candle but to stay low and watch them cross.

It is the man from earlier, the woman, and them dragging a third man by his arms. She moves more fluidly on the sand, stronger, more assured than her man, even. But now she appears to be wearing a black skirt I didn't notice before.

They don't stop moving, but she gives looks in my direction, her eyes always catching some light to reflect back like a wild animal. They head toward another dock, one oddly not surrounded by shacks. A bridge from warehouses to the ocean, yet no boats sat in the water, and nothing stored above.

I crawl along, still following, not exactly sure why I feel so compelled. I could turn back, get help, rush them. I still followed.

The woman and the unconscious man disappeared. The sleazy man began to come back toward our shacks. His gait was odd now, too, but not so stilted like the woman. This was someone who was tired or drunk, winding their way home by memory and instinct.

When I confronted him in the open sand, the wind forcing us to raise our voices, he wasn't defensive or suspicious at all.

"What were you doing; what did you do to that man?" I asked him.

"Hey," he says, his eyes alighting with recognition. "You want to see something amazing? You really won't believe it."

He looks around, then smiles wide. "I have no idea how I got here, but what was happening before this was better than any woman or home-cooked meal, friend. Please, you gotta let me show you!"

He doesn't wait. He's turned back toward the dock he came from, faster than I can grab at his arm to stop him. As I find myself forced to give chase, I can hear him humming an indistinct tune.

We reach a concretion of oceanic detritus under the dock. It seemingly supports a portion of the woodwork, but it was here from long before. Swirls of shells dot the surface. Creatures long dead, trapped for eternity. A hole at the base is big enough to crawl through, and the woman's hummed tune echoes up from underground.

"Go on." He says, his smile wider and wilder now.

I'm afraid of him. But not that he's going to do me harm, not with his hands anyway. He seems stricken with some sort of madness. What I'm afraid of is that he is lost, and maybe a victim himself.

"What's down there?"

He hums.

The two tunes and the breeze begin to sync, and I feel a compulsion to investigate the hole in the rock. One step, but then revulsion. The tune is suddenly out of sync. I'm free of compulsion, but the man is now swaying in ecstasy.

I look at the hole again. Even though I can see it, see that it descends into the ground, that it's big enough to fit through and maybe explore, I am certain that it's impassable.

"I think there's something in the way." I say.

"No, it's okay," he assures me. "You'll love it down there. Full bellies and happy thoughts only. You'll know nothing but satisfaction, friend."

"You go down." I tell him.

He does not argue. In fact, he does as I tell him as though my words are his own thoughts. He continues to hum, and the discordant duet keeps me locked in place, but he moves. Nothing keeps him from

49

stepping down, then crawling lower, and disappearing into the darkness below.

The humming continues for just a moment. I realize that the darkness that I see in the hole moves. It isn't dark down there. Something darker than the absence of light had been at the bottom of the hole, and it had taken the man. His humming is gone, and I can see a rocky floor. He is gone, too.

The barrier I could feel keeping me from descending has lifted. It isn't an invitation. Again I can feel the urge to go get help. I step out onto the sand and draw breath to shout for security, for police, for anyone awake, but realize the wind will swallow up the loudest I could ever call out. There are no other lights in the shacks, anyway. Sleep has descended on the Jungles. And who would come to my aid anyway? I've trusted no one.

The humming begins to ascend from the hole again. His voice; only his voice.

Trying to get help could lead to his and the other man's death. Going down myself could result in three, but maybe I could save someone? Indecision doesn't help at all.

I take a deep breath. An awareness overwhelms me it might be the last time I smell the salty Pacific. The scent of men living in squalor hanging in the air for miles. Smoke from treated wood that shouldn't be burned. Cooking meat that shouldn't be eaten. And the underlying fragrance of rotting fish that haunts every coast.

My first foot is in the hole. Then I'm in a cave. The air doesn't move down here, and the smell of fish is intense. I relight my candle.

I am surrounded by large lobster traps, big enough to hold men. Many do. I examine one closest to me and see the man is alive, sleeping, *smiling* in his sleep.

The man's humming crackles from behind me, his vocal cords unable to hit the deep notes he's trying to reach. I turn to find him lying on the floor, further into the cave. The darkness beyond darkness churns behind him and hums the tune much deeper and clearer than the man can.

A tendril of the darkness grabs the man's leg, pulling him deeper into the cave, into the absolute blackness.

I step forward again, my candle providing enough light to bely the darkness's physicality. A glint of movement, there is slickness to the surface. The lack of color full of form covered an area too large to be a creature, not one creature, it couldn't be just one…

The eyes open and blink nearly in front of me, closer to me than I realize the thing even was. Eyes I have seen before.

"I like your light."

Warm and cool air rush my face.

෨ೲ

Waking up, I am lying down. I turn but feel that my space is limited. I am in one of the lobster cages. The rope netting is tightly woven, and I have no leverage to meaningfully pull at the knots. A tarpaulin covers the cage to keep me dry, but a tiny hole lets water through.

I brush my hands together to rinse them in the slow, but steady drip. I sniff at it. It doesn't smell rancid, so I hazard a drink with cupped hands.

The woman with the too large eyes is outside of my cage looking in at me. She pushes a bowl of what looks like seaweed from the beach through the rope netting, then mimes the act of eating at me. She sits and places the candle in front of my cage, but out of arm's reach. She won't give me my own means of egress. She lights it, then covers her face like I had when I prayed.

She begins to hum her tune again, into her hands, not praying at all.

When she looks up, she smiles too wide, matching her too big eyes. She pets the ropes of the cage.

She calls me her pet. She looks around at all the cages. The men she has trapped have all become her pets.

A FEAR MORE THAN REAL

ATG

I picked at my palm, the dry skin there flaking and itchy. My palms had sweat so much the last few days that they were in some dual state of being dripping wet and painfully dry. Even as I sat there waiting in the restaurant for my friend to arrive, my nerves got to me. I could see the tiny beads of perspiration forming.

It felt as though everyone looked over their shoulder at me—leering. They couldn't know anything. But, sitting by myself, obviously nervous about something and staring blankly into my hands… I'd probably steal glances at that individual myself. I traded one nervous tick for another as I started to scratch at the odd bald spot on my neck.

I'm 35 and living a decent enough life. I've got debt, but I make my bills. My longtime girlfriend Sasha, her daughter, and I live in a house instead of an apartment. We're the picture of a family unit. Except for the last few days that is. Later in the week I have an appointment with a psychiatrist, but I have to talk about this thing *now*.

So I called the one friend I know would keep a secret no matter how big or bad. It was probably a mistake to meet in a public place, but I needed a drink. Pretending to be sober for my family made for very little alcohol at the house.

I saw Jason as he came in, greeted by the hostess. As I waved, he returned the gesture and pointed me out. The perky, young girl nodded and Jason meandered between tables until he reached me next to a planter full of trees and grasses. This restaurant had an open air sitting area in the middle of the place. The warm sunlight pouring in and the smell of vegetation was slightly relaxing, but *only* slightly. We shook hands, I had dried myself on a napkin first, and the first thing he noticed were my two glasses filled only with melting ice.

"You doing all right…everything okay at home?" he asked.

I had stayed with him a few nights during a particularly bad spate with Sasha. I shook my head, "Nothing like that."

The waiter slipped by and greeted his new guest, asking Jason his drink order.

"Uh, two of whatever he's having; I'll get this round." Jason smiled as he sat.

As the waiter left, I shook my head again. "No, everything at home is fine. *Great* even."

"*But…*" he urged.

I beat my fingers against the table in rapid succession. How do I say this thing? How do you frame something so terrifying, yet questionable? My finger taps turned into knuckle wraps. He stared worriedly.

I leaned forward against the table. "I think I *killed* somebody."

I felt sick saying it out loud. Literally sick. My stomach turned and a belch full of bile rose in my throat.

Choking it back, I continued on. "I'm *sure* of it actually. I remembered it the other day. It was so vivid…"

The waiter came back with our drinks and asked if we were ready to order food. I leaned back in my chair. I could sense a burst of cold sweat along my brow. My armpits uncomfortably moist, I tried to rub them dry with my shirt against my body. It was warm, surely others would think I was just susceptible to the humidity.

Jason ordered a sandwich and I asked for an order of fries. Before the waiter had even left the table side I was sucking on the straw of my third Long Island.

"Dude, slow down!" he hissed as the waiter stepped away. "What are you talking about? Did you hit someone?"

"*No!*" I nearly shouted.

Anxiety was getting the better of me. I could feel my legs vibrating. I shook my head. It seemed shaking my head in a constant statement of *no* was all I had been able to *do* with my head.

"No." I continued. "When I was a kid. When we were in middle school."

Those words came almost naturally. It seemed after getting the initial admission done with, the rest was willing to just have out.

"Like, toward the end of the school year." I went on. "The last day we had to dress out for gym. When we were done with class, it was just me and this other kid. For, *whatever* reason, I had a plastic fork…"

The thought of it made me feel sick again. I could feel that fork in my hand again and with it the intense sweat in my palms returned. His eyes shifted to my throat where my Adam's Apple was bobbing as I swallowed too much saliva to speak through.

The look on his face was one of confusion, but also rapt curiosity.

A ragged sigh escapes before I go on. "He didn't see it coming. I don't know where the thought came from, I don't remember if we were even friends; I just stabbed him in the throat. The prongs broke, but I cut the skin. He stumbled back into his locker and I struck again. That time the broken end sunk in and his blood gushed out over my hand."

Grinding his teeth, looking like he was chewing on something, he scowled. Not in disapproval, but disbelief.

"It was so hot." My voice hitched in my throat.

It wasn't from sick, though. I could feel the fear and emotion tensing every muscle, making the bottom of my jaw and entire neck feel constricted. That thick tightening that precedes wailing.

I held my right hand up, where it quivered at the wrist. "My whole hand was drenched in his blood and it was hot and it stank; but I remember just pushing in more. His eyes were terrified and he tried to grapple with me but he was already dying. There wasn't any other sound but his initial falling into his locker. We were on that back row, no one would have seen anything unless they went looking. I washed my hands and left him there."

Now Jason was shaking his head. "What are you even talking about? Where is this coming from?"

"I remembered it. Just a few days ago." I sighed again. "I've been sick with it ever since. I haven't told Sasha anything, she just thinks

I'm bothered with stress from work. But as soon as that memory flooded my brain, I've been wracked with guilt. I can feel the remorse…I can feel the *fear* of dealing with the consequences! It's *real*."

He took a long sip off of his drink. "No. That's not real, that didn't happen."

His denial shook me.

Fear turned into urgency. "I can feel his *blood* on my hand."

It was then I noticed his skin had gone pale and he had finished his drink in two turns. "That didn't happen. You're wrong."

"Jason, I'm telling you," I pleaded. "I *remember* it, it's so vivid and clear. I *killed* that boy."

"Do you remember it in the news?" he barked.

"What?"

"We still had a few days of school after our last suit up in gym…do you remember an announcement of a kid killed in our locker room?"

Now my head swam. The more I thought about it, the pieces started to slip away.

The waiter broke the silence delivering our food. Jason tore into his sandwich much the same as I had started drinking before the waiter made sure everything looked satisfactory. I gave a weak smile and thanked him.

My plate of fries sat there becoming the only thing I could focus on in the entire world. A peel of steam rose up despite the midday warmth. My jaw quivered as disgust stayed my hand from even attempting to eat.

Jason on the other hand was voracious. He looked like he couldn't wait to be done and on his way.

"Jason." my voice sounding much calmer than I felt. "I did it. It happened. I probably blanked out a lot around that event; I only *just* remembered it. I can feel it in my *gut*. I know it happened."

He puts his sandwich down, his chewing slowing. Picking up his glass he drains the gold colored remnants at the bottom of the glass.

"That didn't happen…not like that." He winced with the last.

55

Cold realization washed over me. Was he confirming my new found fear?

"What do you know?" I breathed.

He didn't look me in the face any more.

"Jason?"

"You didn't kill anyone…you never stabbed anyone."

Was he right? Was this some ultra-realistic nightmare?

"You didn't do it, because…" he continued, working his jaw again as he paused. "Because I did that to *you*."

The cold remained, but now a heat filled my ears along with a sound like rushing water.

"*I* stabbed *you*." He moaned. "*I* left *you* for dead."

The hand I swore I could feel that mystery boy's blood on reached to my neck. I rubbed at the spot on my neck that wouldn't grow hair.

"I don't know why." He shook his head. "Hormones. Curiosity. It was sheer luck I didn't get caught. You were so out of it for weeks after that, you couldn't remember what had happened. Any time anyone would even mention your stay in the hospital you'd become irrationally upset. So your parents let you keep thinking nothing had happened. They had no clue I did it and asked me and our friends to never talk about it."

The nausea in my throat changed. The fear of being caught went to the fear of being confronted by a monster. Death felt imminent.

I could smell my fries. Without much thought I picked one up and shoved it in my mouth. It tasted both wonderful and disgusting. If what Jason said was true, it exonerated me of my own fears. Though now I was faced with someone who had the ability to murder and he had exercised it on me.

I rapped my fingers in quick succession on the table again…right next to my fork.

"So I don't have to worry about being…*caught*?" I asked.

It sounded selfish.

"I guess not." He conceded. "I guess that's *my* fear now."

I ate another fry. "Are you sorry? Do you feel that gnawing at the bottom of your stomach? Like you've got an urgent need to visit the bathroom?"

He huffed a nervous laugh. "I…yeah. Yeah, I do. And I *am* sorry."

The waiter came back around to check on us and asked if we wanted another round. I was two and a half in, but barely felt anything. Of course I had drank them quickly. I picked up my glass and tilted it toward Jason.

"You want another?"

There was a nervous smile shaking its way across his face. "Sure. On me again."

"Okay." I look back at the waiter. "Drinks on him, food is on me."

The waiter smiled and retreated.

"So…what now?" he asked.

His face and posture belied a nauseated terror. That was probably how I looked before he came in the restaurant.

I thought a moment. "That fear I've carried the last few days—of having taken a life, of having to pay for it—it was worse than learning my best friend had tried to kill me once. I imagine it's the fear that you're grappling with now."

His nod in the affirmative was small, but fervent.

"It's like when you're little and you've done something minor but someone says they're going to tell on you."

His brow furrowed again, there was the nervous laugh as well.

"You live with that fear now. But I'll still drink with you." I said raising my glass.

He stared at his food with the same disgusted disdain I had previously given mine. But my fries and drink tasted better with every passing bite.

MEASURED AGAINST THE WALL

ATG

It is wartime and you are in a prison camp. High concrete walls create a perimeter with thick forestry surrounding. Pockmarks along the height of the walls suggest heavy gunfire from within. A trench is being dug out on the inside along the walls. It's winter, the topsoil looks frozen solid. The smell of wet earth contrasts the frozen air.

"Why a trench on the inside?" a companion wonders beside you.

He is unfamiliar to you.

You say, you don't know.

"I mean, there are already walls—what are you trying to keep in?"

"Me?" You ask.

He nods in appreciation. "That's a fair point, I suppose."

A guard yells something and motions for you both to follow. Another guard follows behind.

The sky is a slate of gray clouds. The sun's position is impossible to place. You have no watch on your wrist. If it is morning, afternoon, early evening—you cannot tell.

The camp seems silent. Beyond your own movement, you hear no other prisoners, no guards conducting drills, no barking dogs. Wind does not disturb the trees.

Among closed warehouses, a concrete bunker entrance stands open at the center of the compound. Metal doors lay open exposing stairs. The guards continue marching you down into the earth.

A dim yellow lamp lights another guard sitting behind a desk at the bottom of the stairs. He could be bored, stoic, resigned. The other guards show no emotion, either.

Their uniforms are generic, no ranks, no names. Yours has your name while your companion is missing any identifying information. You are dressed against the cold, but are not warm.

On the wall behind the desk are ticks drawn in pencil like those measuring a child's growth. After some banter with the escort guards, a language you do not understand, he signs you in on a ledger. You know he's written your name, but the lettering seems wrong. You know the word is right, but it aches to try and read. Before you can resolve the dissonance, you're marched to your cell.

There's little light after the entryway. Your companion and you are deposited into a cell together. As your eyes adjust, you see two other cellmates, like you, dressed barely warm enough for the cold. There are no bunks, only the floor and walls to rest against. A communal bucket to relieve yourself sits at the back wall below a small window vent to the outside. The guard locks the cell door and leaves without a word.

"Well, this is depressing," your companion says. "I mean, yeah, you've imagined us in a prison camp. You must feel guilty about something. I wasn't expecting the Ritz by any means, but c'mon! We have to sleep on a dirt floor?"

"Don't worry," one of the other two men says, though which one is unclear. A ventriloquist throwing their voice between the two of them. "They execute us at dusk. You might not have to sleep tonight at all."

"That's cryptic," he responds and looks back to you. "Why dusk?"

You protest and ask how you should know.

"Because this is all in *your* head." He states as though he knows it for a fact.

You tell him to stop, to shut up and leave you all alone. Sleep might be your only escape in this place.

He holds up his hands in surrender. Then he makes a motion like he's zipping his lips together to overemphasize the point.

You each take a corner and sink to the floor.

"Though," he starts again, "since it's your mind we're trapped in, if I speak it's because *you're* knocking at that door."

You ignore him.

"Here you ask 'what door?' and I explain, 'Why, the door to the real world!' And that's what I'm here for. *Knock knock!*"

He nods at you, expecting the typical response.

Folding your arms, you stare at him.

He looks to the other two, but gets no cooperation from them, either.

He blows a raspberry and leans back against the wall.

"I've got a really good one of those, too. Well—you do, anyway."

You are thankful when he shuts up for a while.

Maybe some hours pass before a guard pushing a cart stacked with platters stops at your cell. He sets a tray with four bowls balanced on the slot in the door. One of the other inmates grabs it and sets it on the floor, taking one of the bowls for himself. You claim your own.

In the unwashed tin bowl sits a crust of what might be bread no bigger than your palm and a moist gruel that has no smell. This may be your only source of nourishment; you try to eat it quickly. Your throat is quick to close and refuse the offering, instead sending a convulsion straight to the pit of your stomach. What tastes like the snot at the end of an infection sits in your mouth. Your struggle with spitting it out or swallowing the mouthful whole only succeeds in making you examine the "food" with every tastebud.

"Your mouth is thinking for you," your companion says as he sniffs his bread. "You could spit it out and be done with it. Or swallow it and keep it in your body. If you spit it out, it's done, but you're left hungry; if you swallow it, who knows what horrors lie in the future."

Managing to relax your throat enough to swallow the mouthful, it goes down in one, painful gulp. It threatens to stick in your throat, but you can feel it slowly compress and slide down, hitting your stomach like a rock.

"Hey, man," he shrugs, "you see this through as far as you feel necessary. But I'm here to tell you it can end. *You're* the one in control. If you would just wake up, this nightmare could be over."

No one speaks. You don't tell him to stop it and the other inmates don't lash out. An execution may lie in your future and apathy is already settling in.

The gray light through your tiny window dims as daylight eventually gives way to the night. There's a clatter of metal somewhere, some footsteps, but you can't tell how many men or how far they've gone. The silence stretches out.

You only notice that you were nodding off when the distant crack of rifle fire startles you, reminding you: it is wartime and you are in a prison camp.

The other two men give you withering looks then return their attention to their own laps. The man making a nuisance of himself stands up and crosses the cell to look up through the vent. You know he can't see anything revealing, but he examines what little bit of overcast sky he can see.

"If we're all inside your head," he says looking down to you, "and someone dies, I wonder if that's like losing a memory? Do you feel like you've forgotten anything? Like, 'there goes the piano lessons'?"

You groan, responding with frustration that you do not play the piano.

"Ah!" He beams. "But maybe you did and now that's gone. You know what? Maybe you're not asleep. This *is* all in your head, but maybe not a dream. Maybe you've been knocked unconscious, you're being choked… Or maybe you're drowning! You'd better come-to quick, before more of your memories fade!"

You point out someone has lost their life, you suggest he stay quiet, at least out of respect.

"I'll observe a moment of silence for those precious hours in front of the piano lost to the murky depths."

You grow impatient with your continued wakefulness.

❧❀❧

When your eyes open, you are greeted by a roach charging toward your face. You lurch up from lying on the floor and stomp the thing as though it might be able to hurt you. Cursing the embarrassing outburst, you prepare for the inevitable teasing. Instead, there is silence.

Morning light forcing its way through the vent reveals that you are alone in the cell. A few more roaches gather around a tray on the floor. Breakfast must have already been served. You wonder why you would be allowed to rest through the morning. Were the other prisoners taken outside? Divided into different cells?

Swiping away the roaches you chance eating the hard, stale bread even they seemed to ignore. You listen beyond the sound of your working jaw, trying to hear other prisoners, the guards, work outside…*anything*. Either you're alone or no one has the will to so much as sigh aloud.

"Hello?" you call out through the bars.

There's a sound of distant brushing, like heavy cloth being dragged across concrete, but no perceptible response. You can't be sure of where the sound came from. This bunker could be this one cell, the hallway, and the encampment above. It could be a labyrinth. You have no frame of reference.

As the weight of uncertainty threatens to occupy your mind, the sound of metal doors echoes down the hallway. Shuffling feet make their way toward the cell.

Despite his annoying insistence on the unreal, you're relieved to see the nuisance still alive.

You ask where they had been.

"Does it matter?" he asks in return. "It's all in *your* head. Why don't you tell *me* where I've been? I'd be interested in that since I'm your construct."

He's committed. You think he shouldn't be here. Maybe he should be in a hospital.

You look him over. He's picking at the edges of a busted blister in the palm of his hand. No one has had a shower in days, everyone is a mess, but the dirt under his nails looks fresh. Sniffing, you can smell the earth on him.

You guess that they were digging in the trench inside the walls.

He bunches up his bottom lip and nods approvingly. "Obvious. But it makes sense. It's not like they have us do anything other than dig or die; so far as you know, anyway. Guess if I came back that doesn't give you many options to choose from, does it?"

As the others filed into the cell, the guard closed the door, locked it, and headed back down the long hallway. No one else spoke. The guard didn't tell you to expect anything, work *or* food, not even cursory grunts.

"See, you got caught up in formulating my response," he says, indicating the two other men. "The more aware you become of this all being in your head, the less your subconscious can do the work. They can't even complain."

You look at the two men. There's sweat on their brows from the hard work, but it's so cold outside you're surprised they're not already shivering.

One meets your gaze, though says nothing. They're like the guards, average men. Were they the same men from the night before? Could you recognize them again if you saw them in the future?

"It's like when you dream and you find yourself focusing on something." The nuisance attempts to explain. "When you wake up, you can't tell anyone what color your shoes were, or if you even *had* any. The focal point is all there is. Your subconscious is giving up— or breaking down. Well, I mean, your subconscious is *you*, but the involuntary part; you know?"

You shake your head refusing to entertain him further. You ease back down along the wall to sit like the other two.

"It's a lot of work keeping up an imaginary world," he says.

You attempt to distract him away from yourself and ask him to reveal his name, because you don't know it since it's not on his jacket. You won't carry on with him anymore until he reveals something about himself.

"You'll figure it out; I'm sure of it. I've got faith in you." He sits down. "I don't really have a choice but to have faith in you. You're my creator—that kind of makes you a *god*, doesn't it?"

You scowl at your knees.

He slips into the corner opposite from you and wags his finger.

"That's a thing to consider, really." He starts. "You've created all of this. But you believe in God, right? I'm able to bring it up. Someone up out of your sight created you. Who's to say God doesn't have a creator?"

"God is eternal," one of the other two men says.

You both look, but neither have raised their heads. Nor do they look like they've spoken. Their faces are expressionless. One of them even breathes deeply as though asleep. The ventriloquist effect again.

"Okay!" the nuisance says, raising his hands. "See, that's your subconscious resuming a bit of work. A little lazy for my taste, but making sure your beliefs are defended, trying to get yourself back into the groove of your creation. 'It's not just the two of you!' it says, 'This is the real world!' But which one said that? Hmm?"

You look over at them again. They are the embodiment of exhaustion.

You declare that you are tired of his talking.

"So much for not talking to me anymore, I didn't tell you my name! Besides, do you even know what time it is?"

You flash him a rude hand gesture before folding your arms close to your chest.

"Do you know what the origin of that sign is?" he asks.

You sigh, regretting the relief you felt upon seeing him return.

"I mean, I know you do. If I know it, you must know it. But have you ever really *thought* about that? Here's this whole world history with little nuanced bits that can pop up as necessary, but how do you know any of it is real—real to the really-real world?"

You would rather be asleep, even though he is correct that you do not know the time.

"Do you ever think you make it up in just that moment?" He drones on. "Like this world's entire history, every minute detail, is created and fleshed out, supported by whims. It's like any of it only exists when you need it to."

You cover your ears as he continues to talk out loud about how much of history you could have created. Ancient history, pre-history, geological history; how many stars can you imagine? Because that's how many would be in the sky. He is incessant.

The afternoon comes and goes. So-called *dinner* is served, and you choke down more gruel. He prattles on about how he's disappointed you're willing to punish yourself. When the light from the tiny window is nearly extinguished, you hear a staccato burst of gunshot. Multiple executions.

He gains your attention. "Can you remember your dad?"

❧

The light is different, and you're curled on the floor. The disorientation unsettles you. Sitting quickly upright, you kick a few pebbles across the dirt floor. You realize you were awake and acting out before you were fully aware. No one stirs. There's the faint sound of heavy breathing; the others are asleep. Thankfully, the nuisance breathes the heaviest, nearly ratcheting into a snore.

You think he's drained himself fabricating so much nonsense.

Your eyes gloss as you realize that sounds like something he would accuse you of falling victim to.

"Mm-hmm," he mutters in his sleep.

You freeze, thinking he has responded to your musing. He smacks his lips and shifts his shoulders, making the same sound again.

You finally breathe, releasing a grateful sigh.

It doesn't keep you from fearing his psychosis is infecting you.

Leaning back against the wall, you stare up at the window. The edges are bathed in pale light. There is no point of light cast on the floor. It is nearly pitch within the cell, save the faintest sense of a lingering green haze.

You pull and flex your fingers against the floor, feeling dirt and grit as you dig ruts below your palms. Then you feel some*thing*, buried just beneath your left hand. Scooting over to give both your hands room to dig the item out of the floor, you reflect on how you had been laying when you awoke: fetal position, lying on your right side, this spot just below your knees. A crusty piece of cloth breaks free.

You shake it out as you stand and raise it to the window. The light is barely enough to make anything of it. Your disbelief gives you pause. You stare at it, hoping your eyes adjust and reveal an alternative truth. Like the ledger when you were checked in, you know it's correct, yet, alien and wrong.

It's a name patch. Yours is frayed and faded, but still in place. The problem, however, the name is the same as yours. Down to the raised lump where the sewing machine must have jammed for a moment. The lump has the loosened center you pick at in times of boredom and stress; it even fits the groove of your fingernail.

You look at *him*. You can only see his form.

Everything in the cell is a dark form. Except, one of the other two men is missing. You wonder when he was taken or if he's coming back; or if it'll be another unrecognizable, insipid prisoner of war, resigned to their fate.

Stepping as lightly as you can, you cross the gap between yourself and the nuisance. Details come into view, wrinkles of cloth and the rise of his body with breathing. His chest is towards you. You can envision the frayed box on his left breast where a patch had been. You start to hold the patch out toward him, to see if it would fit, but pause.

Maybe you happen to share a name. You may have received your uniforms from the same manufacturer and the machine always messes up that letter in that way. Stranger things could happen… Regardless, was this even his? The area of his missing patch could have changed with wear, removing probability that this would fit, or even contributing to a dubious match.

You inch closer. Arguing with yourself over incredulity you pause and lose focus.

He reaches up and grabs your wrists. You gasp, struggle, and fall on your rear. He doesn't let go and neither does your shifting weight disturb his position. His eyes are wide open, though dark.

"Why do they shoot us at dusk?" he growls.

He doesn't say anything else, and you can't be sure he's looking at you. A nightmare and you were in reach?

You say nothing and wait for his grip to loosen. His eyelids slide back shut and he lets go. Folding his arms into his chest, he shifts his body and makes that same *mm-hmm* sound.

You stare at him a while longer. The dusty nametag with your name sewn into it is clutched tightly between your two hands, still ready to place it against his chest. You don't move. Everything he has said up to now has seemed like a game; something he has cooked up to pass the time, awaiting his turn to die. But, why *do* they perform the executions at night?

Why doesn't anyone else attempt conversation? You never hear sound from the hall. When you were brought in, there weren't curious whispers. No one made a peep, not guard nor prisoner, to wake you for breakfast or a day's work. Everyone is afraid to make any sound—except for him. He won't shut up.

Was the missing cellmate executed or did you *forget*?

You tell yourself that's dangerous thinking, shaking your head.

You can't succumb to that madness. That's what *he* is: insane. Driven there by the situation, the war—maybe he always was.

You back up into your corner. Balling the dirt crusted patch in your fist, you lean against the wall and wait for dawn.

☙❧

Words.

You look up to see the guard. You don't know what he's said, but you can guess what he's saying. It's your turn to get up and work. The light through the window is bright and silver. You won't be shot, not under execution circumstances anyway. Just follow directions, even if you don't understand them.

That this guard said words at all brings relief from your midnight stress. Maybe a couple foreign words, but it's better than unintelligible grunts.

Looking around, you're the only one in the cell, save the guard urging you to get up. It's still silent. No sighs, clearing of throats, nor coughing. Your footfalls barely echo against the concrete walls.

Reaching the corner, there's the desk with the ledger and lamp, but no guard. Your escort scribbles something indecipherable. Climbing the short flight of stairs, you pass through the frame of the open door. There is no one to be seen or heard.

The guard says something else. It sounds like a different language this time. Every time they speak it's unfamiliar.

You look at him, completely at a loss.

He shoves you and shouts indecipherable words.

You tell him you do not know how to respond.

He rolls his eyes and grabs you by the shoulder, shoving you along a path worn out in the frozen earth. You round a supply building, or what you guess is one for all the barrels you see through the windows. You see the trench is nearly complete and the two mostly quiet men from the cell are there digging.

Pickaxes and shovels lay just outside of the trench. Either anticipating more workers or because they often break against the hard earth.

The guard shoves you again.

The word he says is again babble. Either he knows several languages and is trying them out to see if you catch on or you're so exhausted you just don't recognize anything anymore.

Getting the general idea that you're supposed to work, you grab a pickaxe.

You ask your partners how long they have been out here.

They say nothing.

The guard only watches long enough to see that you start working before disappearing around the warehouse. Like another roach waiting for the lights to go out, the nuisance comes from the other side of the building and jumps down into the trench with you.

"I bet you're wondering why there's only one guard," he says, sliding down against the edge of the earthen wall. "And why he didn't notice that I was gone when he brought you around."

He produces a cigarette, and while you don't see him light it, he continues on with the thing smoldering between his lips,.

"I bet you're wondering why he's still here, too."

Smoke puffs out with the words and he points his thumb in the direction of the previously missing man.

As you offer your thoughts that a guard could have moved him, it strikes you, how did *he* know one of the others was missing at all? You push the thought away. He could have awoken when the guard opened the gate; his head was nearly against it where he had slept.

When your attention finally returns to him, he's grinning like a schoolboy looking at something inappropriate

You tell him he looks deranged.

Attempting to work, he soil is rock hard at ground level. It's exposed to the cold and what little water resides there freezes solid for a couple feet down. Once broken through, though, it's as soft and loose as any garden in spring. It's when the frost melts from the heat of your bodies and the floor turns to mud that the work becomes taxing.

"Yeah, yeah, that's it," he says behind you, sounding as though he's just gulped a drink. You look over your shoulder to see him only flicking his cigarette. "Keep up the internal monologue on digging the trench. Focusing on one thing gives you a chance to add more detail, keep up the farce a little longer. You know it's going to fail, though, right?"

You say that you already know it's all in your head.

"You mock, but…" He pauses a moment. You can feel his eyes boring into your back. "Isn't there something you wanted to ask me…?"

Had he really been awake when you thought he was having a nightmare?

You set the pickaxe at your feet. Turning your shoulders enough to frown at him, you reluctantly dig into your pocket and feel the stiff patch. Before pulling it out, your finger finds the mar in the lettering.

For a moment, you wonder why you're here. You wonder why he's here, why together? Where is *here*? Where are the sounds of war? Haven't you been at war all this time?

You pull the patch out and hold it up in his direction. You tell him it's not a big deal that you happen to share the same name.

"True to your word, though, you know my name now and we're talking again."

You turn back and continue to dig at the softer dirt.

He harrumphs.

You throw the shovel down and turn on him once again.

"You didn't notice?" He smiles. "You're so preoccupied with keeping some sort of balance that you've come to just accept anything that's in front of you? Except, the truth of it all, of course."

You beg him to stop being cryptic, to stop antagonizing you.

"You set down a pickaxe, but just now you were digging with a shovel."

You look at your feet, and there is indeed a shovel there.

You must have switched tools when he was talking. He is intentionally distracting you for his amusement.

Before you turn back around, you can see him shaking his head, and you know he's going to continue.

"Rationalizing is tedious." He says. "It's a dream; try for something more original."

You notice the pickaxe against the trench wall. Without leaning, he wouldn't be able to see it. There's also a second shovel drowning in muddy water.

You pick it up and show him the evidence.

"Then tell me my name."

You feel your left side tingle. A chill oozes down your spine and the feeling of electrical arcs radiate out along your ribs and through your muscles. You nearly drop the pickaxe.

You say it's yours.

You know what he's going to ask next and the thought of having to answer nauseates you. You think of when he claimed the executed were parts of you, that maybe you would have forgotten something with their deaths…

"Then tell me *your* na—"

"Get up!"

Standing above him a guard speaks familiarly, however accentless. "Get your ass back to work. No more breaks. Next time I won't give you a break, then you can shovel your own shit!"

There is relief, but you know what the nuisance is going to say with this new development. The problem being, you don't know if you can disagree with him.

"Mighty convenient." He smirks. "Looks like the old fabrication's still got some defenses left."

"Shut up and get to work."

For a moment you think the guard has spoken in your own voice. But, you both said it at the same time.

The guard turns to leave, and the nuisance laughs and makes finger quotes, mouthing the word "coincidence."

Digging goes on for what feels like several hours before you break through and meet the other side of the trench. With the work completed, you suspect the encampment's population is about to drop sharply—and shortly.

When you look up to the wall from inside the trench, there are bullet holes but no signs of blood, of executions. Everything about this place inspires odd questions, but everything has a seemingly reasonable explanation. High bullet holes, surely, because some men could not bear shooting their victims. A trench dug inside the walls, reasonably, to capture and quickly bury dead bodies. Executions at dusk because…

You continue to stare upward. With the constant blanket of dull clouds, time remains impossible to figure. It still seems like morning, but work must have gone well into the afternoon.

A guard speaks from behind.

Back to the odd language you cannot place.

"No point in trying," the nuisance says, looking up to the guard.

The guard sneers and beckons you all to crawl out of the trench.

"You don't know their language, so you string together foreign words you've heard over the years…" he says. "But that guy spoke earlier and you understood. Aphasia setting in, maybe?"

You guess the guard told you to get up so you're getting up.

You're marched back to the cell.

"So, I guess we're really getting to the end of it," he says, and you file back into your cell, content to ignore him.

The silent two collapse into their corners. You plant yourself firmly in the center of the single shaft of light. It could still be mid-day, you realize, regardless of your position relative to the sun's traversal. How long were you out there?

Taking a corner, you acquiesce to your plight. Sitting in silence, more countless units of time slip by. Minutes? Hours? Days?

You have gone mad.

That is what is happening. You have no watch to keep time. When you look out of the vent, there is no sun to gauge its position in the day or stars and moon at night. Cooped up with two men resigned to their fates—their souls checked out before you ever entered this place—and a third so far gone that his method of coping is to hope that this is all someone else's fantasy that can be woken up from. You realize madness is your only logical option. You stand somewhere between broken silence and raving lunacy.

A bulge tightens your throat, but the unease does not upset your stomach; instead, tears burst from your eyes. You summon what little might you have left to keep the sobs locked deep within your guts. Burying your face between your knees and the wall, you hope to fall asleep.

You feel the question in your mind, would death be better than this vague existence?

❧❦

For the first time since entering this place a cacophony of voices breaks the silence. Orders barked in more languages. Shouts of shock, anger, resistance, pleading, and fear. There are men crying. Many call for mothers and mercy. You're reminded of battle. The desperate yearning to return *home* is palpable. The air stinks of it, and your own emotions dare to join the milieu.

The nuisance grabs you, like he had in his sleep. He's in your face, his breath smells like a dog's. "None of this is *real*, you must wake *up*!"

There is no time to argue with him. A guard yells several words, each sounding like a different language in rapid succession. Rushing you out, you're met with a crowd, a *crush* of bodies being marched hurriedly through the narrow hall. Where had so many men come from? A concentration camp? The march forward is rapid, and there is little time for curiosity.

Prisoners and guards bottleneck at the opening of the bunker, guards measure the inmates against the walls, marking ticks along the tops of their heads. Counting numbers and heights, they're yelling at each other over the rising roar of the condemned. As the door comes into view, four lines are formed, routed to a particular wall of the fort. Was the trench wider in some areas to catch the bodies?

Distant, concussive cracks interrupt the sound of men yelling. This is a mass execution.

Questions swirl and fall against the shock at how many have erupted from the darkness. How could they all be so quiet? How could you not have noticed any sort of tell-tale signs that a larger population existed here? No coughs, no shambling bodies, no grunts from prisoners, or orders from guards.

"All your synapses are firing!" the nuisance says, continuing to answer questions you have not asked aloud.

You can't fathom how you heard him.

"Your brain!" he yells. "It's on fire! It's now or never. You *must wake up!*"

You reach one of the guards measuring the inmates. Shoved against the wall, a pencil is dragged across the top of your head. You remember the kitchen door and your mother.

The cracking grows more rapid and louder over shouts of fear and pain. The fear seems to permeate everything—not just prisoners, but the guards, the walls.

"Actually—I'm kind of eager to see what you've cooked up for us, if I can be honest," he says into your ear, his urgency dissipated in favor of morbid curiosity.

There's nothing left but to play along, you point out he should already know if he's a figment of your imagination.

Both of you are shoved toward the same wall together after guards holler over the din.

"The subconscious and conscious minds are separate from each other," he says. "I do know that if *you* wake up, all of *this* will end. You could save us all a lot of pain if you would, you know?"

There's a smell in the air. Blood, mud, and gun smoke. It is familiar and terrifying. You are reminded of that first night's dinner, relieved and reviled.

Guards stand at every visible corner, there is no option for retreat. One man tries, as the thought barely crosses your mind to run, and he is shot down. You can't see anyone with a weapon raised that direction. Snipers?

Looking up you are greeted with the first clear sky you've seen in what feels like years. Putrid green stars boil in a pitch-black veil. The moon is unfamiliar; too big and threatening to drop to the earth. Smoke from the rapid firing guns and exhalations of fearful, dying men *must* be distorting the sky.

The staccato explosions resume, not from gunfire, but from beyond the walls in the woods that surround the compound. You think allied forces could be zeroing in. Their march so urgent the trees are bending to their will. Hope dares to flutter in your heart.

73

"I wonder what it will feel like when you wake up?" he asks. "Like, do we just wink out?"

You tell him someone is coming.

"Probably your mother." He nods. "You can hear her out in the hall. Ready to come in and wake you for school, no doubt."

You tell him it isn't a joke, to listen.

A guard aims at you, and you raise your hands, shuffling along in line toward the wall.

"No, of course not." He agrees. "School is very important, I believe in a proper education. You should go ahead and get up now, then. I bet your breakfast is getting cold. Or coffee if it's your spouse?"

Reaching the trench, thick boards offer passage to the other side. The men along this wall are within inches of height of each other. Anyone who falls either quickly scrambles up one side or the other, some being shot for coming up too fast on a guard. Bodies are already piling into the self-dug mass grave.

An unusual mix of sounds in the woods cause prisoner and guard alike to pause and look blankly upward. Hope tries to convince you that it was tank wheels. Fear hears something incalculable.

The dark outline of trees, visible only by where they mask the stars, sway and lurch as *something* makes its way toward the fort. Urgent orders and frightened yelps resume as the guards force the death march onward.

"All right, a bit scary for my taste," the nuisance says as you cross the boards. "I would personally appreciate it if we could bring this to a close. If *you're* going to insist on seeing this through, I implore the writer above you to cut this out!"

You find yourself surprisingly disappointed.

"Well, *you're* not cooperating!" he says to your downturned face.

Barely enough earth for your feet is all that keeps you between the wall and trench. Across, your executioners. They look bland. No insignia denotes country, no ranks. Every rifle is different. A hodgepodge force in a nonsense fort.

You wish they would just have done with it.

You hope it *is* a dream.

The guards all point their rifles skyward as green smoke billows over and begins to engulf the crowd. It is cold, but feels thick like humid, summer air. Chemical agent from the incoming forces?

"Knock knock," he says staring across the trench.

The weird air tingles in your mouth. You're shocked he's still playing at his game right before death.

You relent and ask who is there.

"Spell."

You already know the punchline. Is that what he meant when he said *you* knew the joke? The ruse finally given up?

But he doesn't spell "who" after you ask. He make's unpleasant sounds like flesh tearing.

You look to him but are disturbed by a sharp pop that seems to wrack his body.

He begins to slump. Turning his head, there is a hole where his eyes and nose went through the back of his skull. The green mist coalesces into wormy tendrils that probe the gaping wound.

His body falls forward, but never hits the ground. The mist comes together and solidifies around his body like a snare, whipping him up into the air and over the wall. Turning away, you see the same fate befall other bodies from the trench. Guards shoot wildly, at prisoners and at the unknown.

Directly across from you is a guard with his rifle leveled at your chest, though his eyes are locked on something high above. It strikes you: they shoot at dusk because *this* is what comes. The bullet holes high in the wall are shots missing their target of what threatens from beyond. The trench is here to catch bodies, but not to bury. It is a distraction. A feeding trough.

Craning your neck you see translucent green tentacles, filaments, and feelers, all searching, but nothing reaches for you. *Is* this a nightmare? Is this the culmination of madness before execution?

You squeeze your eyes shut. Attempting to recall a quiet life before the war, to remember a warm bed, you find they are not there. It is all static in your brain. The surrounding horror continues to grow louder, and you are left living to hear it. So many men dying.

It is wartime and you are in a prison camp.

You plead with yourself for it to be a dream.

The swirling black and red behind your eyelids turns to green. All sound fades to a cotton-muted, distant memory. The ground disappears from beneath you. You realize your existence has only ever been here. You were no soldier sent to a prison camp; you've only ever been a prisoner. Fibers of the mist force their way under your skin, prying flesh and ripping muscle from bone. The pain is a fire working along every nerve ending, contrasting exposure to cold air. The pain is something to be cherished, for it will end.

Opening your eyes, you see the gaping maw of that which lies outside the walls. It is mist, smoke, and smog. Teeth, fangs, and broken bits of bone. It is earth, trees, and bodies of mysterious men, and it is ravenous, focused only on you.

The lump in your throat forms into words, beyond ancient and foreign, merely shapes of sound. It is an animal's cry of certain finality. You speak without thinking, your last words somehow not even your own. They are words beyond understanding, a language never meant to be spoken, and though you don't know them, you know they are spelled in letters that hurt to see.

THE SHADOW ON PITCH

THW

I recently acquired a sheet of super-black material. Think: thick paper, 99% light absorbing. I framed it without glass to hang on the wall. It's a fathomless pit, a portal into utter darkness. Shine a flashlight? Nothing, just black. Wave your hand in the beam? No shadow. Reach out, touch the material and your brain makes you think it should pass through, yet there's the wall. It's unsettling, but fun.

Except, one day there's a shadow.

Every day I tested it, thinking my brain was playing tricks on me. Then, I started seeing it even without a light. No one else could, but when I checked, there stood a reflection only in shadow.

I became obsessed with checking, like it was a mirror and I watched myself.

Then I noticed it was no mere shadow. It no longer matched my movements and was often there before I approached. It started to take form, develop features. It was no longer my sheet of paper coated in light absorbing material; it had become an actual hole in my wall. Something on the other side looked through. Worse still, it began to look like me. Then it smiled.

I tore the frame down, ripped the material to shreds, and tried to put the hallucinations behind me.

The shadow wasn't done with me. In any dark place, I could see him. Darkened hallways, in the night beyond cars' headlights, even in simple shadows, there he was. Always smiling. Now, beckoning.

I've been locked in my home for two days, sleepless. Every light's on, every door's open, lanterns lighting corners behind furniture. It's only a matter of time. Soon I'll close my eyes. No matter how many lights are on, sleep will come. And there will be no escaping the shadow in pitch dark.

THE EVIDENCE
ST

A man whose badge reads "Pascal," so I only call him Pascal, delivers an item to me. I catalog and store evidence collected through years of routine law enforcement.

"Hello, Pascal," I say. "What have you got for me today?"

I never give him the option to say "hello" back. I have learned that despite my own name being on my chest, he has never returned the pleasantry. He does not want to converse, not with me, which is just as well, we both have work to do.

Today, however, Pascal lingers over the small brown bag with the evidence stamp information filled out.

"You know those shanty tenements down by the docks?"

They're beautiful stone apartments with the misfortune of having industry replace commerce as their neighbors. They may be considered "cheap" by some, but once they were the place with the beautiful view of the bay.

"One of 'em burned down." Pascal says. "They're saying a boiler malfunction. But the whole place is white ash—just the one building through, damndest thing."

It's a startling statement. "They're *stone* buildings, Pascal, how can the whole thing be ash? You mean the masonry caved in?"

"No!" He says excitedly. "That's what I mean, *everything* was reduced to ash. There's nothing but a square hole in the ground where the basement would have been, full of ash looking like snow."

He upends the bag and the chalk-white object hits my desk with a quiet thump. He doesn't know what he has, just that it was the only solid object found among those ashes. He cannot tell that he has activated a weapon.

I can, though. Seeing a written language triggers familiarity. If one sees words they know, they will read them.

I pick it up, reading more.

"Only thing left." Pascal says, distantly. "The brigade chief wants to call it an unfortunate accident, but no one died, they all got out."

He says it as if disappointed, then scoffs out, "That's mighty convenient."

I may have countered it's a *good* thing nobody was hurt, but I hear the written words in my head much louder.

He calls them "fishy caravanners," despite they were living in a well-built structure that apparently disintegrated. He reasons either the landlord or the tenants set the blaze and it got out of control. Some sort of fraud or evasion—a coverup. All said with evidence concocted in his head.

He didn't believe their stories. They smelled burning meat amidst a black smoke that didn't seem to affect their skin or clothes. That the fire itself was impossible to see, as black as night but as hard to look at as the sun.

"Maybe one of 'em crawled into the boiler with a bunch of their weird trinkets and *that's* what burned the place down. Worthless, all of 'em. One less building, maybe they'll go back to wherever they came from."

Weird trinkets…wherever they came from. He has no clue and he doesn't care to learn.

The device looks like a spool carved from pumice, small enough for one's palm. The latticework of stone around dimples is arranged to be read, if the language is familiar, and conveys a history.

Once upon a time, there was a city beyond a mountain, and beyond that, a sea of stars that never ended. The city had a king who could be many places at once. He fought a disease that took all his people until only he remained, and his ability to be many places was all that was left of his society. He became everyone, and with so many of himself, he labored over how to defeat the blight that destroyed all he had once known.

81

In any war, there are measures taken in extreme duress, experiments that go too far. Weapons are made from practical intentions. A cleaning tool pushed too far, meant for disinfection of small areas, but given a radius and effect much greater enhanced.

I have never seen the waves of the black sea against the shores of that old and forgotten city. But I know the smell of hatred. And I know something stirs within the dark when we're not looking.

Pascal does not feel anything, but comments on a strange smell in the room.

"It smells like burned meat," he fails to recall what the witnesses described.

There is an instruction on how to activate the device upon priming it. A process begun by my reading its surface. An active bomb in my hand, a weapon against a monster that may or may not exist. There are no instructions for disarming it.

I do not want to.

Pascal's eyes go first. Opening his mouth to scream only releases smoke and a darkness that is indeed too intense to look at directly.

I have learned the language of the city beyond the mountain, but I am not one of its people. I cannot see into the depths of that faraway sea. But I come from *this* side of the mountain, that "wherever" the others came from, and my name would have told Pascal that.

I suspect, however, Pascal *did* know, and thought he could intimidate me with cursed objects and disdain for the dislocated.

Pascal could be *a* monster. The weapon is being operated correctly and eliminating only what it has been fired upon.

I watch him collapse into himself, the uniform erasing itself from his blackening body as it too burns in flames I cannot see. His body becomes rigid, though he does not fall to one side or the other. His tendons snap and his arms and legs fold in on themselves, bending him to a kneel, his head falling to his chest. A contorted genuflection.

Black char gives way to white ashes, form lost in moments. Whatever flame and smoke consumed him left nothing smeared with soot. So focused and small, given only a single threat to eliminate, the floor was unharmed as well.

I placed the device back into the evidence bag and put the bag into an unoccupied locker near my desk.

I was sweeping the last of Pascal's remains into a dustpan when a captain from upstairs came looking for Pascal.

"What happened here?" the captain asks.

"Knocked my ashtray off my desk by mistake, Captain." I lie and hold up one piece of a broken ashtray I have never used, but someone murdered their spouse with. "It's been about an hour since Pascal delivered the evidence from the fire down by the docks. He just dropped it off and went back upstairs."

I tap Pascal's ashes into a waste basket next to my desk while the captain nods and inhales deeply. Could he smell that ocean of stars?

"Shame about those tenants." The captain says. "Glad they all survived, but…"

"It is quite sad." I agree. "But they're a resilient people, they all are. And they have their ways of dealing with hardship."

"Admirable, really." He says.

With nothing left to say, he offers me a good evening—by name—and leaves me to my tidying up after Pascal.

EYES FOR SEEING
ATG

"Before we go in," the nurse said holding a hand up to stop me, "you're going to want to stare at her eyes. Don't."

She continued as I raised an eyebrow at her warning. "It is unsettling and bizarre, but you must push that aside and talk to her like you would anyone else. She may seem catatonic, but after rigorous testing, we are certain she can see and hear. Her brain activity registers emotional response—though, there are peaks and valleys. She responds well to a calm, steady voice."

I frowned. "I need to speak with her about what happened. Will that be triggering? Should I ease into the topic and see how she responds?"

The nurse shrugged. "I can only suggest remaining calm. I know you need to do your job, but I need to do mine as well, and that's keeping our patient comfortable."

"Okay," I said. "I think I understand. I'm ready."

The nurse shook her head. "No. You're not."

She opened the door, and I followed behind her.

Doctor Brianne Toomey was quarantined. Not because of anything contagious, but to protect her from prying eyes. Her room was in an empty surgical wing and within the room an isolation tent surrounded her. She was looking away from the door, so I did not immediately see her face. That was, perhaps, a blessing. I could ease into seeing the results of the incident, or so I tried to convince myself. I knew as soon as I saw her eyes, things would change.

"Dr. Toomey," I said. "It's Jacob Rush, from the lab. I'm here to discuss the incident with you. Well, rather—I guess—I'm here to debrief you."

Dr. Toomey took a large breath, as though she were about to say something, but remained otherwise silent.

❧❧

$t1+AB/C<=(AM+BM)/C$

Dr. Toomey stared at her whiteboard. There it was, an equation to capture the difference between reflection and reality, along with all the necessary settings and criteria she would need to capture the moment. Light bouncing from a subject to a mirror and back again to the subject with a camera in between to catch the disparity. It was not simple. A lot of trial and error, false positives, and mostly disappointment would surely follow. But the settings were in place. The camera rig, looking like something from the set of a science fiction film would begin clicking away, taking thousands of photos at once of an entire scene, albeit a very small one.

If her own image (A) could be captured blinking by the camera (B) *before* a change in the reflection in the mirror (M) was registered *by* the camera, then—theoretically—the camera should capture an instant (time, or t1) where her eyes were open and the reflection's were closed, and the timestamp on the photos would indicate an instant where both images were true, but so miniscule, otherwise imperceptible. Until now. *Hopefully*. The speed of light (C) and the distances she was dealing with were magnitudes smaller than the millions of miles in space where light from the sun was eight minutes old on the Earth. Here it was greater than the blink of an eye, typically 3 or 4/10ths of a second—it was orders of magnitude greater.

If she could capture a moment where the real world and the reflected one were off by a beat, it would have huge implications for the transmission of data. Hidden or extra information could be conveyed in the space between action and reception. The military and scientific applications could be limitless. What was hidden in stray beams of light from the cosmos?

She fired up the camera rig.

The first test, which lasted just a few seconds as Dr. Toomey stood six feet from a mirror with the apparatus clicking away looking at her, the mirror, and both at the same time. For the thousands of photos she just took, it would take extensive examination of images and comparing timestamps, a scientific game of "spot the difference." She didn't expect any results with her first test, but the algorithm tasked with finding photos with the exact same timestamps yet different photo compositions spit out two results immediately. *Surely* an error…

The first set of photos seemed like her eureka moment, she stood with her eyes closed and the mirror image's eyes were only half-closed. It was the result she was looking for! She cheered sitting at her computer, then eagerly opened the next set of flagged photos. This…these? It had to be a mistake. The image was impossible.

∽∘∽

I pulled up a chair. I had seen the photos, knew the results of the experiment. Seeing blurry digital photos was one thing, but seeing her in the flesh, seeing her eyes in person—even if just from the side—was something else entirely. I could feel my stomach in freefall, the anticipation of a drop more than the drop itself.

"Dr. Toomey, I know what happened, but we're not sure how…"

She turned to face me, a reaction I didn't expect. Her eyes—*her* eyes—fixed on mine, daring me to engage. All the fear and panic I had ever experienced in my life came crashing into my guts. I looked down at my feet. She didn't say anything, but I could feel her gaze on me nonetheless.

"The closest we can come up with is the Observer Effect, but that's just thinking out loud. Of course, seeing and knowing a thing can influence its outcome, but that's usually reserved for something so small as a photon particle, not—well, in a way you *were* dealing with photons, but…"

I looked up, out of habit, to make eye contact with who I was conversing with, but here, her eyes, they didn't meet mine. She stared through me, to something else, an inch behind me. I wanted to look over my shoulder to see, but knew I really wanted to see how far the door was. The nurse was right, I wasn't ready for this. I'd seen accidents in the lab, working with scientists who played with light sometimes lead to burns from lasers, but this was something else…

I couldn't shake that phrase: *something else*…

"What—do—you—see?" her voice croaked.

She hadn't spoken in upwards of two days.

The nurse, standing on the other side of the tent, looked at Dr. Toomey in alarm. I'd nearly forgotten she was there. She rushed out of the room, shouting.

"I—I see *you*." I answered.

"No." Dr. Toomey said, stretching out the O into a sigh.

"I see your eyes." I corrected. "It's all I can look at."

"And—what—do—*they*—see?"

❧

It *had* to be a glitch. There were so *many*. What had she captured? Dr. Toomey stared at the image on her screen not knowing exactly *how* to process *what* she was looking at. She quickly bolted to the mirror and checked her face; normal. Her eyes were normal, her nose was normal, her mouth and ears and hairline and cheeks and—it was all normal. What the hell had the cameras caught? Was it motion blur? A deep breath or exhalation caught and the speed at which the shutters clicked captured the myriad movements as one?

Running another test would take no time at all, she had already done all the hard work setting up the apparatus. Thousands of more photos. No results. Thousands more. *Thousands* more. She couldn't even replicate the *desired* result. It *must* be a glitch. In a way, the glitch had forced her to temper her expectations and reign in her excitement. She should be *thankful* for such a bizarre image, it made her think more critically.

But the sight wouldn't leave her mind. The *eyes*…

Dr. Toomey couldn't dismiss the sight. Not with time and separation, not with a glass of wine, not after a night's fitful sleep. She became frightened to even look in the mirror, any reflection for that matter, so disturbed and worried she would see it again, on her own face with her own eyes.

She called in sick to the lab where no one was the wiser just yet. She knew she couldn't hide from the world forever because one test had gone haywire. The following day she dragged herself to work. Her reflection seemed impossible to avoid, though, in the bathroom, on the black screen of her phone, in windows, and once finally back in the lab, *the* mirror.

That had to be it. The glitch was a combination of camera tomfoolery, a fault in the mirror, her own subconscious movements. She couldn't replicate it, so it *had* to be an error. Why couldn't she shake the anxiety of even looking at her reflection then?

"Absurd." She chastised herself.

It wasn't real, no matter how unsettling the result had been.

She forced herself to stand in front of the mirror and examine both it and the reflection it held. No ripples in the glass or grime on the surface. She examined the cameras, looking for a hindering fleck of dust. *Clean.* She scoured connections and ran disk cleanups on her computer. Everything was in perfect working order as far as she could tell.

In a final act of trying to regain control of her own concerns, she looked at the offending photo again. She double-clicked the wrong photo by mistake, but what opened only further horrified her. The glitch was present, when she knew it hadn't been before. This should have been a normal photo of her with her eyes closed. She opened several in a row, all now corrupted. That must be it, something was corrupting the data.

❧⚬⚲

Flustered, but wanting to capitalize on this moment of lucidity before nurses and doctors crowded the room and forced him out, I thought about how I should respond.

What had they found out in the wake of the incident? What did she know before anyone else did? No one had run the test since, so there was only the physical evidence and so many photos with so many glitches that couldn't be explained.

"You see what we cannot." I said finally. "Either because we don't have the ability, or we choose not to."

"You—are—guessing." She said.

"Are you *here*?" I asked.

She blinked. Something so simple, so quick, just 3 to 4/10ths of a second, yet it was the most disturbing thing I had ever seen.

"I—am—*everywhere*."

❧❦

Every photo, hundreds of thousands, ran through the algorithm, every last one had been corrupted and made exactly the same. All with that hideous glitch, all a monstrous approximation of her face. She stood in front of the mirror, too close to run another test. She was examining herself. Looking at her forehead and temples, she wondered what was hiding just underneath the skin. What would cause such a gruesome visage?

She began to scratch her forehead, then she took scissors to her flesh. If it was there, she would tear it out.

She found them, all hiding, but all there. Eyes, so many eyes.

❧❦

I could see the makeshift eyelids that had formed from the cuts in her skin. The nine eyes, speckled across her forehead like a grotesque spider, could look around independent of each other, or they could focus intently, threatening to pop out of their newly formed sockets.

She could see with greater clarity and intensity than anyone else, and it was driving her mad. I could see the fraying threads of her sanity behind her *normal* eyes, pleading with me to do something, *anything*, to deliver her from this new existence.

"I—have—seen—an—*opening*—Jacob." Her voice was distant. "I—captured—a—moment—where—space—and—time—do—not—meet.   A—seam—in—God's—skin.   I—pried—it—open. Every—possible—outcome—in—every—single—choice.   They—are—all—within—us. All—we—have—to—do—is—open—our—eyes—to—see."

I had backed away from the tent as she sat up in bed. She began to scratch at the IV was stuck in her arm. I could see an angry welt forming under the tape. A welt with the distinguished shape of an orb underneath.

"We—are—all—panopticons—of—choices—just—waiting—to—be—seen."

And as she revealed another eye in her arm, I could feel an urgent itch under my skin. Under *all* of my skin.

"*Knowing*—will—open—your—eyes." She promised. "You—*will*—see."

BELLIGERENT MADNESS
ATG

I'll agree with you that the first part sounds like a crackpot, conspiracy theory. How can you take anyone seriously when their first point of contention is the proliferation of scented waxes? But when I get into trans-dimensional unified field theory, that should grab your attention. Let's never mind the sudden growth in popularity of scented lamps and knockoff candle-warmers and seasonal aromas that the consuming public can't wait to get their hands on. Let's stick to harvesting energy from another dimension.

Okay, yes, that sounds crazy, too, but it's not something I made up! Look up quantum computers and zero-point energy. If we were to tap into the energy of another dimension, it would be a miraculous boon to our energy needs. But what if that other dimension tapped into *ours*? Fed on some energy source we produce and got their free energy by breaking the barriers of multi-dimensional space before we figured it out ourselves?

Hmpf.

Okay. There goes that look again; how does that have anything to do with aromatics?

I'm what is called a *high-taster*. I'm exceptionally picky when it comes to food and smells because my olfactory senses are more sensitive than your average individual's. You've smelled something so cloyingly sweet it smells *bad*? Antifreeze, Hydrogen Cyanide, common house paint. Of course, there are people who like those scents, but no one of sound mind would go in for a taste. Well, those types of scents will turn my stomach. That's why when the Scently craze exploded and everyone had three or four of those things in their houses, cars, at their desk at work—I was in hell.

Remember in the 1990's when incense and fragrant oils made a big comeback? New-wave, hippy revival type shit? Used to be hippies were covering up the smell of weed or their own B.O., but now it was just cool to have something burning in your room that smelled like balsawood or patchouli. I shudder to even think about it. But this wax shit, you could make it smell like anything and last for days. You want your house to smell like cheesecake, fresh laundry, and a rainstorm? We've got it all! It permeates everything, there's no escaping it.

My boss thought it would be a great idea to start putting out fresh cut fruit every morning. When oranges were on the table, I could barely make it through the day. So, I took to putting a little dab of petroleum jelly just under my nostrils. I had to! Nothing too strong or smelling like food, just something to block the nonstop assault of designer fragrances.

Then I started to see them. As I acclimated myself to the constant barrage of different scents, I started to see the hooks coming from the back of people's heads.

No, *of course* I thought I might be hallucinating due to my self-care. That's why I stopped and tried to tough it out. But once I had seen them, there was no *un*seeing them. I went to a doctor, I went to a shrink, and when they could find nothing wrong with me and started giving me the looks, you're giving me now, I shut up about it.

Not everyone had them, not then, anyway. Every so often, I would see someone with this slimy, pink hook jutting from where their skull meets their spine—yeah, high up on the neck, you're touching yours, now.

I don't know the mechanics of why you can't feel it, it's from another dimension, maybe they don't want you to feel or see it…

Yeah, the royal *they*, that counterproductive, catchall phrase that makes me sound mad. Well, I *am* mad. Embracing the madness was the only way to stay sane.

But what else can I call it, or them—whatever or whoever *they* are? I'm not the only one and that's why you're here. There's a little diversity in what other people see, but the M.O. is about the same, right? People who claim they're especially sensitive to smells resisted the growth in popularity of scented products then started seeing spikes, tentacles, barnacles, hooks, cords—whatever—something sticking out of the back of people's heads. That part's undeniable and you're trying to find out why. I'm *telling* you why: we're being fed on.

There's something to do with our sense of smell in particular. Maybe an induced synesthesia, you *smell* the good things, you don't *see* the bad things. I'll tell you this, people that have it seem calmer and more even-tempered than the average bear. It's like you're being placated, it's symbiotic in nature—unless you refuse it, like others and I have.

To deny it, to refuse it—and you *can* refuse it—is to court insanity. Everywhere I look is nothing but living hooks and cords. Humanity has been turned into a living engine and all I can see is the exposed guts. Whatever it's taking from you, it's also giving you a false sense of sanity, probably so you *won't* go mad, like me.

And here we are, *the* question. How did I disengage from my hook? It wasn't easy. That's how I know it feeds you sanity and to take it off means madness. I could see more and more people getting hooked, as it were, as I saw it, day by day. Pink hooks, maybe a foot in length, and no one the wiser of their presence; save me. Then one morning I saw mine, in the mirror as I brushed my teeth.

I close my eyes as I brush my teeth, I kind of like the smell of spearmint, and that's when the trap was sprung. I got lost in the moment, focusing on that sharp, fresh smell and the task at hand. I go to spit, look back in the mirror to check my face, pink hook coming out of my own head. I couldn't *feel* it, just see it. I reached back and only felt my hairline, but I could see it, plain as day.

I knew if I could see it, knew that if I was seeing it on other people, then it was *there*. There had to be a way to detach from it. I'd broken the spell of being blind to it, I could break it from the back of my head.

I started looking into other things that are both there and *not* there. Gasses were where I got my idea, we breathe a mixture of gasses produced by living bodies, the earth itself, water, et cetera. There are ways to harvest and consume gasses. Even though our atmosphere is *mostly* nitrogen, it's oxygen that is the key ingredient that gives us life. It feeds other things, too, like fire.

Victims burned at the stake didn't really burn to death, see, the fire consumed all the oxygen and those poor people died of suffocation before they ever burned.

Fire is also what we use to kill off bacteria and germs, other things that are there without you seeing them. Maybe this thing was like a germ or bacteria, and I could kill it with fire. I had no intention of killing myself, but fire doesn't exactly obey. I meant to just get as close to the fire with the back of my head as I could. I did swab myself down with alcohol because it burns quickly. I just needed a quick burn to sever the connection. But, yeah, I burned my whole head and people thought I was trying to take my life.

I'll tell you this, though, it worked. In setting myself free, I saw so much more of what this thing was. I could see that it wasn't just a foot long, but immeasurable. It and so many others, coming from so many different heads in all directions were all feeding into a point high up in the sky. I couldn't see where it terminated, they all just went *up*. I thrashed about in pain from the fire, but also from *feeling* the thing dislodge itself from my skull. The complacency it was feeding me was now corrupted, negative feedback, sending me spiraling into insanity and it recoiling into the heavens.

Maybe it was me screaming, but I swear I heard it scream, too. I saw the thing quiver, all these miles long cords vanishing into the sky. I had broken free, and I wouldn't be the first. Being able to see it all now, I could see it shiver at times and I knew there were others who had figured it out and broken free, too.

Unbelievable, I know it. We're a species that demands evidence, to see is to believe, but can you see the air you breathe? Can you see the microscopic mites that live on your face? Why is it so hard to believe that some interdimensional technology isn't feeding on our brains with hooks that you just can't see or touch?

Because they blinded you through smell. What's that cartoon bird, say? "Follow your nose"?

As more people have become aware, the stronger the campaign to blind us has become. It's not just wax warmers now, it's stronger air-deodorizers, it's scented air conditioning add-ons… Vaping? You have these assholes blowing cotton candy-smelling clouds in all sorts of venues and there's no avoiding it.

I might be scarred, but look at my medical records. If all I did to myself was burn my head, why do I have a circular abrasion on my cerebellum, yet no corresponding trauma on my skull?

I'll keep my madness, thank you. I live in a world choked with tentacles climbing to the sky. It ain't pretty. Somewhere up there is a gaping mouth with all these proboscises syphoning *something* from us. Sounds great, right? But, at least I know I'm not food for the gods. Can you be so certain that you're not the one going insane with all this free calm? Can't you feel it? It's irrational, everyone is too docile.

Yeah, you're touching it. It's there. The more you become aware of it, the less of a grip on you it will have. Keep talking to those of us who have all gone mad for eerily similar reasons, with eerily similar concussions. You can't argue that I haven't been concise. I might be locked up, medicated into a stupor most of the day, *for my own protection*—pfft! They just don't want me trying to liberate anyone else. The ones I did free have done nothing but thank me.

PANE
ST

At the corner of Fontnot and 36th there sits a little dress boutique. For five generations the Osterman women have passed the shop from mother to daughter; not once moving, never faltering in sales. Over the years, their craft and handiwork have only improved and grown more desirable. Though hardly world-renowned, their dresses, blouses, and slacks are sturdy, functional, and aesthetically pleasing. Their accessories, however, have afforded them their lucrative longevity.

"Supple leathers and finely polished bone adorn our broaches, bracelets, and bags." So went one of the more successful advertising slogans of Osterman's.

Priding themselves on the same look and feel of exotic skins and ivory, they meticulously craft their wears from cattle hide, bone, and horns. In more recent years, that fact went hand in hand with an environmentally conscious assurance that their materials were locally sourced, homegrown, grass-fed, free-range cattle. Nothing went to waste. The Osterman's were a constant cornerstone of the economy and model citizens of the community.

Inside of Osterman's, the décor has remained largely unchanged since its construction. Heavy, dark colors line every surface. Wood stained almost black. Paneling of green and gold. Converted gaslamps pump out oily amber light. The counter, looking like it was constructed from one solid piece of wood, is lively with swirling flowers and leaves carved into its edges. On the back wall behind the counter there hangs a large, murky mirror with a subtle, if noticeably cheap, frame. However, its simplicity adds to its charm, contrary to its surroundings. But against the old world darkness, the clothing pops.

Frilly, patterned dresses come alive, shining brightly against their dim surroundings.

Preston Mall, the building there at the corner, has been the site of a hotel, restaurant, numerous specialty shops, and recently a bank and an art-house movie theater playing classics on the weekend. All of them neighbors to the Osterman's themselves since the building's construction. Half of the second floor belongs to the family, serving as their home and studio. With a grocery store in some form always within a block of Osterman's, it's no surprise the family is rarely seen about town.

Despite the non-mystery of a family who lives where they work, longstanding rumors have become the stuff of urban legend. The building is said to be haunted by tortured spirits, their pained moans audible in quiet times. They bang against the walls, as if beckoning to be let in (or *out*) from just the other side. Osterman's in specific is said to have had the most activity.

"We call him Bram," says the girl at the counter to the spooked customer looking over purses.

The shop was quiet after the initial tinkle of the doorbell and her customary greeting. As the young man looked around and spotted a display wall of leather handbags, he crossed the shop, his footfalls sounding too loud in the silence. He looked self-conscious, embarrassed by disturbing the peace. She let him peruse at his will. Upon his picking up a shoulder bag, though, a sharp pop of wood sounded throughout the shop, loud enough to produce an echo. His shoulders jumped up to his ears, and she stifled a laugh.

Relaxing, or at least forcing himself to loosen, he offers a quiet laugh. "These old buildings, hunh?"

Nodding in agreement she comes around the counter. "Fryer's down the street has this one spot toward the back corner that acts like an echo chamber," she says. "I swear it sounds like voices inside of your own head if you catch it just right. That always creeps me out. But Bram doesn't scare me, he's just obnoxious."

Smiling half-heartedly, he looks back to the purses.

As she approaches, she sees him tense up. "So, are you looking for your girlfriend...or wife?"

99

"Uh…no," he stammers. "My—my aunt, actually."

"That's sweet." She says through a smile. "Do you know what she likes in a bag?"

"Um, she's one of those that carry a giant bag full of everything she could possibly need," he groans. "She's always wanted one of your purses, but she never buys anything for herself." He pauses, hesitating a beat too long. "She's coming to visit, and I wanted to surprise her."

"Aww, I bet she's also one to refuse anything too fancy," she says. "Like, maybe insist on returning it if she thought it cost too much?"

"Exactly," he chuckles. "But I won't let her. I'll tell her if she takes care of it right, it'll be the last one she ever needs. You guys make some quality stuff from what I hear."

"We certainly try. We do have simpler choices, though."

Pulling what looks like a black bowling ball bag from a hook, she says, "This one has brushed nickel trappings, instead of the bone. Won't scuff or come off as easy. We take pride in our accoutrements, but let's face it, the threading gives after so long. Our more affordable selection is actually some of our most durable, and I bet she'd be more willing to accept that notion."

He smiles and takes the bag to inspect it. "Aren't you supposed to upsell me? Convince me the smallest, most expensive thing is in my best interest?"

Shaking her head, she states matter-of-factly, "We sell to our customers, not the register."

"Well," he cocks his head toward his shoulder, "you guys' have been around a long time, so I guess you know what you're doing."

Nodding as he turns the bag over in his hands, opening it to look inside.

"I'll trust your judgment, then." He says. "I'll take it."

"Wonderful!" she smiles. "Let me get you a box to present it in and I'll get you rung up."

As she steps through to the back, he walks to the counter and stares at himself in the large mirror. An urge to retreat sends a shiver down his spine, but he remains steady. Brushing his fingers through his hair, he pauses as he hears hasty tearing of paper and a couple of dull thuds wracking the back wall. A more distinct *bang* seems to erupt from the mirror itself and startles him again, but she's back in the shop before he can even commit to a reaction.

He gestures toward the box, deflecting his embarrassment. "I hope it wasn't too much trouble getting that…"

"Oh!" she looks down, then waves him off. "No, I accidentally pulled the next one in the stack down and it tumbled across the floor, no big deal."

She boxes the purse and runs the register. He pays in cash. They exchange pleasantries as he slides the box under his arm, but before he can turn to head toward the door, she stopped him.

She bares her teeth in an over exaggerated grimace. "This is going to be awkward, but I have to ask…"

He raises an eyebrow.

"Would you be interested in getting a drink, with me…sometime…" she flushes and looks like she had regrets letting the words slip out.

In turn, he blanches and stammers, but manages, "Of course! That would be excellent. Uh, so long as it's just us and not any ghosts."

Her color returning to normal, she smiles. "No, and we'll avoid Fryer's, too; so, just us." Grabbing a business card she writes her number on the back and hands it to him. "We close up at five; give me a call about an hour after that. If you want—"

"You can expect it…" He takes the card and looks at her name. "Tamala. I'm Patrick. I guess—I'll—uh, chat with you later, then."

They both smile awkwardly, and then laugh.

"Okay," she says. She points at him, bolstering her own confidence. "I'll expect that call, then, Patrick."

"Absolutely. I look forward to it." He raises the box under his arm. "And thank you!"

They nod to each other, laugh again, and Patrick pushes through the door. Without knowing it about the other, they both breathe sighs of relief and excitement, followed silently by nervous curses.

∾∾

After a light dinner with perhaps a drink too many, Tamala and Patrick walked the Red Brick District. Having a family that stretched back to the city's foundation, Tamala was chock-full of historical trivia, but Patrick wasn't without his own knowledge. He worked in the downtown library and was able to fill in gaps, offer interesting asides, or, quite sheepishly, correct inaccuracies. She didn't seem to mind, though; they were hitting it off and the conversation wasn't dying down.

"Okay," Patrick says as they sit at an outdoor table of a coffee shop, "I have to admit something."

Still smiling, he runs his fingers through his hair, looking anxious.

"Am I sure I want to hear this?" Tamala jokes.

"My aunt isn't coming, er," he shifts on his chair. "What I mean to say is I *don't have* an aunt; I cooked up that story on the fly."

Tamala gives a half-smile and a raised eyebrow.

"I didn't even mean to buy a purse." He grabs his forehead and shakes his head. "I wanted to come in and say 'hi,' maybe ask *you* out, but…Bertrum?"

She chuckles. "The ghost? Bram."

"Whatever it was, it completely threw me and then you were quick with the sales pitch, so I lied and just got wrapped up in—Then you asked *me* out, now I've got this purse I don't know what to do with—"

She reaches across the table, placing her hand flat near him. "I *know*."

"Wha—how?"

"I've seen you around, I remember bumping into you at the library."

He turns red.

"It's okay. I noticed when you recognized me. We didn't even say two words, but I remembered who you were when you came in. I used my sales-pitch to see if you had someone in your life already. It's okay if you want to return it. So, if you're worried about that, don't be. We're out now and I'm having a good time. Let's keep that rolling, okay?"

Heaving a sigh of relief, he still shakes his head. "I must seem skeevy now."

Laughing, she says, "No. I appreciate your coming out with it."

"Ugh, I feel like I need another drink," he moans.

"That can be arranged." She smiles. "Why don't we head back to my shop? I've got wine. I can show you around the interior of Preston Mall. Maybe we'll see *Bram*."

"I'll take you up on the drink and tour, but if I see a ghost, I'm gone."

She beams. "Let's go!"

❧

Along Fontnot, several older buildings hide their bulk with storefronts, belying their true size. A general idea can be gleaned with a reasonable knowledge of the size of the city blocks and where alleys segment the buildings, but Patrick was genuinely surprised, and impressed, with just how much space hid behind Osterman's. Granted, the Osterman's had also lived in the building since its construction, so ample living space should be expected, however Preston Mall seemed to stand deeper than even the movie theater would suggest.

The only sound, besides their chatter and footsteps, is from the theater. A thrum of bass from soundtrack and voices making no discernable words, yet still sounding larger than life, echoes through the barren plaster and concrete. Surely, during the day, the bank makes the soundtrack that breathes life into the emptiness.

"It must be eerie on nights like this." Patrick muses. "I mean, the theater and voices in the hallways. Well, I bet *you're* used to it, but it seems eerie to me."

"It can be." Tamala agrees. "If it's a movie with music or a lot of action, it can fade into the background, you know it's a movie. But those movies that are dialogue heavy, not even horror or drama, just those scenes with a lot of talking, it can get under your skin even if you *know* what it is."

Inside of the loft apartment above the store, the sounds of the theater are even more muted. Just a vibration, felt more than heard. Inspired by the movie through the wall, the conversation had turned to their favorite pieces of entertainment: movies, books, and games. Far away sounds faded to imperceptible white noise.

Patrick leanes forward from the couch to reach for his glass of wine, but dizziness strikes him and his arm feels like a club. Knocking over his glass, he apologized at first, but then stares at his hand.

"Why can't I feel my arms?" he says, almost laughing.

"Because I drugged you." Tamala says, leaning forward herself, resting her elbows on her knees. "It's about time it took effect. I gave that to you almost an hour ago."

"Why would you do that?" he asks. His words aren't slurred, but he feels drunker than he thinks possible. He sees her begin to say something but cuts her off, still on the verge of giggling. "You're gonna kill me. You kill people and use their skin for your purses!"

He knows he should feel terrified, but he doesn't really care. Everything is just on the cusp of being humorous.

She scoffs. "What? No! That's disgusting." She shakes her head, then scoffs again. "Do you really think that? Think we could get away with something like that? Jeez! No. No."

"How come you drugged me, then?" plopping back into the couch, he notices the numbness growing into his chest, though he can still breathe easily enough.

"Because I need you calm and cooperative." She states. "Have you ever heard of a *Pane*?"

"And how come I don't seem to really mind?" he says, slowly trying to finish his initial question.

"Shush. *Have* you?"

"Like a window?"

Shaking her head, she stares into his eyes. "A *Pane*." She says it slow, over-emphasizing.

"What?" he thinks his face should be making a question, but it just feels blank, like he can't convey his confusion. "Those aren't real. That's just a legend."

"Oh-ho!" she laughs. "But they *are* real, I assure you. I have one."

Whatever drug she had given him, the heaviness of his numb limbs begins to lift. He still can't feel, but there is a weightlessness now.

"Inter-dem…dime?" fighting laughter again, he tries to focus as intently as he can muster. "Inter-dimensional windows are just fairy tale."

"Can you stand?" she says, ignoring his statement.

It sounds absurd, why would he cooperate with her? But even without thinking, without wanting to cooperate, he finds himself standing.

"Nice." She smiles, standing as well. "Let's go downstairs. I have something to show you. It's important."

"I think I should call the police…" he says, barely able to force his eyes into looking down at his phone on the coffee table. Some of the spilled wine pooled around it. He wonders if it might be damaged.

"No, that's not necessary." She chides. "Let's go."

In his mind, he tries to will his arm down, to grab the phone and call for help, if it even worked. Instead his body obeys her command and follows her through the apartment.

"This isn't right," he says.

How can he express his concerns and desires, but not feel the actual urgency? Why would his body work against him in such a way? He was a prisoner inside of his own head, just riding a machine at her will, yet, he feels apathetic to it. He knows he should be protesting, fighting, flailing, and screaming, but he feels no emotion and has no choice but to observe.

"No, it isn't, but it is necessary," she says.

Leading him through the door, she locks up, then gives him gentle urges and tactile commands to go this way and that as they go to the store below.

In the storage room behind the storefront, there are dresses, bags, and accessories, either in plastic or in various stages of completion. To the corner, a fallen stack of boxes haphazardly swept into their own area. Behind those, snaking along the wall that would be the wall behind the counter in the store, a series of cables and tubing that don't look as though they connect to anything.

"You know I told you about Bram…" Tamala says, stopping him. "He is real. He *might as well* be a ghost, but I can show him to you."

"I said I didn't want anything to do with ghosts," he says, his words falling flat.

"Oh, but it's important."

She smiles. He can see she's hiding something. Drugging him certainly gave it away, but talking about myths and ghosts as though they're reality while denying she's about to murder him suggests something...*ominous*.

"You know the story of the *Panes*." She states as she urges him to the front of the store. She speaks *at* him, giving him no choice but to listen as she continues, "Windows that gave way to something from outside our world. Well, I have one—*we* have one. My family. Ever since the building was built. They were more prevalent then. There was one in most every building. That was, until the thing came through and there was a consensus that the *Panes* would be destroyed and it would be best just to forget about them. But my family kept theirs. We hid it in plain sight, right inside our shop. Bram is stuck outside and he needs a way in. So, he watches from the store."

She stops him behind the check-out counter, facing the antique mirror.

"The ghost lives in the mirror?" he slurs.

The weightlessness seems to turn back into numbness. His tongue feels too big in his mouth. He wonders if the drug is wearing off.

"Kind of?" she shrugs.

"Is he going to posses me?"

Pulling over the stool she uses to rest behind the counter behind him, she has him sit.

"This is the *Pane*. In a resting state, it can be a mirror—well, act like one anyway. It plays back almost instantaneously what's right in front of it. But, activated, you can see what's..." She pauses to think of a word. "—Outside."

"Outside of what?" he asks. "No, wait...*is the ghost going to posses me?*"

"I don't know." She smiles as though curious and excited to find out herself. "But your other question, that's why I need you calm and cooperative. What I'm about to show you will make *no* sense. Your reaction may be to flee, to scream. I've seen people faint. You get used to it as you look at it, though."

Reaching for the side of the mirror, she continues, "Bram may not be right there right now, but he'll come. He likes you and wants to meet you…the bump, earlier, that got us talking, that was his signal."

"I don't want to meet Bram."

Sliding her finger down the edge of the frame, the mirror seems to just blink away, revealing a starscape. It's not like a television. There's obvious depth and no light emitted from the surface. It's like peering into the night sky. To one side, there's a faint dustiness.

"That's the Orion nebula. Real space isn't quite as colorful as we see in pictures, those are enhanced."

"It's just a picture of space…"

"Oh, you know better than that."

And he does. The depth and dimension are eerie, causing a sense of vertigo. Even though he's firmly planted to the ground, he feels as though he could fall.

"Go ahead. Take a look. You're actually missing the best part."

His body obeys. Now he can feel, though; his numb limbs begin to wake with the firing of pins and needles.

Before he can even cross the gap, he can see that there is land extending to a horizon. The *Pane* is like a window on a structure looking out onto terrain. A terrain that is barren. In the pale starlight, he can only see gray stone and dust, streaked in random places with scorch marks revealing darker tones just below the dust.

"It looks so *real*," he says, reaching his hand up seemingly of his own volition.

The thought occurs to test his capabilities, to run right for the door, but fascination trumps the urge.

Reaching forward, where glass or some type of surface *should* be, his hand passes through. Shocked and immediately panicked, his body remains still, much to his chagrin.

So much for running away, he thinks. The apathy toward the situation remains in place of emotional reaction.

Knowing there should be a wall there, a barrier, causes its own sense of imbalance. He had seen the opposite side in the back room.

"How?"

"It's a *Pane*. They're real. And this is one."

"I thought they were just windows?"

"Well," she leans against the edge to catch his gaze. "Windows can be *opened*."

As if intoned, a cloud of dust lists into view, stirred suddenly from just out of view.

"Is this looking out into, like, *outer space*? If it's really 'open,' how come we haven't been sucked out?"

"Smart! Good. There's an atmospheric membrane, kind of like a static forcefield that keeps all the different environments from mixing."

"All? Plural?"

"*Panes* are basically access panels connecting two or more places, pending there's a network of course. I don't understand the science. I just know this one works, how to turn it on, and that it looks *outside*. Outside of the ship. That we're on."

"That's. . ."

There's no sound coming through the frame, no difference in temperature, but Patrick can feel a sudden change of pressure. The invisible barrier supposedly keeping the atmosphere in stiffens against his hand.

"No, Outside is *out there*," he says, wanting to gesture his hand back toward the street.

"We are on a ship, Patrick." Tamala says, taking his meaning but correcting him. "Or a sort of manmade island. A series of asteroids lashed together that we all live on and in. Something happened a long time ago—disease outbreak, strife, mass hysteria, no one knows—that caused us to cut off contact with the rest of the ship. Why we're all on a ship is even more of a mystery. Maybe something happened to Earth we're unable, or unwilling, to cope with. Almost no one alive in town is even aware anymore, but haven't you ever noticed that no one leaves and no one new comes along?"

"I meet new people all the time."

"It's a big space that we live in," she nods. "People can go their whole lives without coming close to exploring the entire habitat. But a habitat it is. Something happened and now we all live a lie. A pretty well fabricated one, but a lie nonetheless."

"I think you getting away with skinning people for purses is a little more believable than this," he rebukes.

"Stop with that!" she sneers. "Anyway…Bram has been on the outside of the ship. He needs in, and sometimes he thinks he sees someone who can help him. Maybe he knows you work at the library. Maybe you know something that can help him."

Turning his gaze back to the *Pane* he's startled to see a figure standing there. Involuntarily his body goes rigid. He thought maybe he actually felt dread, maybe his fight or flight sense had actually kicked in, but indifference glues his gaze to what he knew he should be terrified of. The figure, though in the shape of a man, Patrick can tell is no *man*. The thing steps forward slowly with deliberate, calculated steps.

"I don't want to meet Bram," he says, his voice still incapable of conveying the fear he knows he should be telegraphing.

Patrick's hand remains against the invisible barrier. Stuck in place, no matter how much he wants to pull back, he has no choice but to watch as the monstrosity reaches up. The fingers and thumb, all looking too long and too thick, reach toward his hand and take hold. Pinpricks of cold and electricity rush through him as either the forcefield gives way or the thing's frozen hand makes contact with him.

"I don't—"

Coming into the low light cast throughout the shop, the thing holding onto Patrick's hand is revealed to be clad in some sort of spacesuit, dusty and patched with makeshift fixes. Piercing the membrane between them, a hiss gives rise to an animalistic howl filling the room. Unable to breathe, Patrick wonders if the sound is the thing, the air escaping around it, or the blood pounding in his ears.

"Only you…" a voice lilts, seemingly from all around them.

Patrick forces his gaze as far away from the thing as possible, and sees that Tamala is no longer next to him. Looking back into where a

109

face would presumably be upon this creature, he sees only more suit cloth. Wanting to scream, to struggle, he only bends and maneuvers in support of the thing.

"If you are Bram," Patrick manages to force out, "I don't know how I can help you."

"…and you alone," the omnipresent voice sings again, now accompanied by far away music.

The suit hisses, venting some interior gas, and opens like an "X" from the head to the crotch and along the arms and legs. Where Patrick desperately wants to look away, to save himself from what horror might be within, he is instead greeted with only emptiness. The suit, however, doesn't stop climbing through the portal and onto him.

Now leaning and bending back over the sales counter, Patrick realizes, without being able to do much more than watch, that the suit will envelope him.

"Tamala?"

The suit tightens on him, sealing him in. Once complete, nothing seems to have happened; short of being sealed into an alien suit and unable to see in the eyeless hood. There was only darkness and the old song playing softly.

"Tamala?" he calls again.

No answer.

He tries to flex his fingers, move his feet, or to even turn his head. Whatever drug she gave him still has its grip on him. Prickles of what he thinks might be his limbs waking again suddenly sends a burning sensation across the surface of his entire body, seeping into his muscles, and spreading throughout his core.

Red lettering appears before his eyes, blurry at first.

BIO-RECLAMATION AND MAINTENANCE. . .

WELCOME, THOMAS HAVERFIELD. MULTIPLE CRITICAL ISSUES IN NEED OF IMMEDIATE EXAMINATION.
. .

"Bio-reclamation?" Patrick asks the void. "This is a…this is a *garbage man suit*? Who is Thomas Haverfield?"

The suit gives no answer, but from without, a muffled voice answers.

"I've never seen it work before!"

"Tamala? What the hell is going on?"

"Bram hasn't ever accepted anyone before! You must be one of his descendants!"

Bram. B. R. A. M.

Terror at the thought of murder gave way to the horror of unimaginable technology and the notion of an imaginary world of lies, to the dread of being accosted by an alien from the depths of space…only to learn it was a suit that just happened to fit him. For all the revelations piled before him, the realization that proved to just be a real kick in the gut was that now that this thing fit and recognized him, he was probably expected to *work*.

His field of view goes from black to what is directly in front of him. Tamala stands over him, beaming with excitement. Dark red letters fill the edges of his vision, unobtrusive, but along the right messages nag him about work orders that need to be completed and systems that need to be checked. Other diagnostic information as well as the name of the song and artist, *Only You — The Platters*, hover to the left.

Not only was he faced with coming to terms that he lives on a spaceship, that they *all* live on a ship, that there was technology tantamount to teleportation, that a symbiotic maintenance suit recognized and *claimed* him, but he was also now a maintenance technician. Despite everything that should send his mind reeling, the mundanity of this lot cast upon him makes him laugh. He was now expected to be a *space*-janitor and it probably was *important* and *necessary* like Tamala had claimed.

Tamala laughed along at first, but was quick to realize Patrick really didn't find anything funny.

Through tears of laughter and frustration, Patrick sighs, "I'm going to return that purse and then I'm going to write a very bad review for your store."

DEBRA

THW

EXT FORESTED AREA NIGHT

Woods. Quiet. But they look a little warped at the edges, like a fisheye lens. Headlights from a car round an unseen road and as the beams come parallel with our view they blind us. There might be the static of an untuned television channel within the flash. The woods come back into focus and we see the car clearly coming up a gravel driveway next to a pre-fabricated cabin.

Parking, two people get out of the car. The driver stares into the woods.

PASSENGER:
It's already midnight! I'm glad this lady was cool with us showing up late.

DRIVER:
She seemed cool. Cute dog in there.

They stretch as they talk, but the driver doesn't stop looking into the woods.

PASSENGER:
Aw, a dog?

DRIVER:
Yeah, little white thing—did you see that?

There's a pause. The passenger is confused and looks over at the driver.

PASSENGER:
What? The dog? I was—

DRIVER:
No, as we were pulling up. I thought I saw something in the trees, glinting—glowing—I don't know.

PASSENGER:
You think it was a ghost?

The driver finally breaks their attention away from the woods.

DRIVER:
What the fu—no! I'm tired, I guess. Look, let's just hit the sack tonight, it's been a long drive. We can get up and take this place in in the morning. I bet there's a rock or something in the woods, I just…

PASSENGER:
Spooked yourself. It's okay. That's why we're way out here. Get away from all of that and just have some time out in nature, right?

The driver pops the trunk of the car and says a defeated "Yeah," as they grab their bags and let themselves into the cabin.

Our view remains outside a moment longer, a square of light blinks a few feet into the woods from the car. Only feet in front of where the driver had been standing.

INT CABIN NIGHT
The pair are already in bed. The lights are off. Their luggage is open, but not haphazard. A whisper breaks the silence.

VOICE:
Debra?

It's distant, and sounds like it's coming through an old speaker, static filling the air around it.

VOICE:
Debra?

One of the sleeping forms turns over, exposing they're the driver. They have a scowl on their face, disturbed, but ready to fall back asleep.

VOICE:
Debra?

The driver's eyes pop open and they look up.

DRIVER:
Did you hear that?

The passenger doesn't stir.

VOICE:
Debra?

The driver sits up and looks out the window behind the bed.

DRIVER:
What the fu—I think I see something out there.

They look over at their sleeping partner who still hasn't stirred.

The driver gets up and slips into a hoodie and some shoes to step outside.

EXT CABIN NIGHT

The driver walks around the cabin and the car to see something glowing just off the gravel driveway, its own light showing that it is buried in fallen foliage and new growth.

DRIVER:

An old TV? That—that can't be working out here…

VOICE:

Debra?

DRIVER:

I'm not Debra. I don't even know if this is real.

The driver puts a hand to their head as they continue to come closer to what appears to be an old cathode ray tube television set left to the elements.

VOICE:

Debra?

DRIVER:

I'm not Debra. This has to be a dream…

They stand and turn on the spot and begin walking back to the cabin.

DRIVER:

I need to talk to—

The light of the television set rises into the air, the sound of wood creaking, leaves falling, and stones tumbling accompany the sight.

VOICE:

Debra?

Cut to black.

BENEATH
ST

I open my eyes enough to see our daughter, Sue, standing beside our bed. She gently shook my arm to wake me.

My voice cracks as I ask, "What is it, sweetheart?"

Dim light from a window bathes her in a ghostly blue.

I blink a few times, trying to rouse myself enough be present for my 13-year-old daughter. But no question was necessary, before I prop myself up, I can see Sue is not alone.

Standing along the wall, the entire length, black-robed and hooded figures, shoulder to shoulder. We're surrounded. I can't believe so many people could get into our house without waking us. My guts want me to shout or scream, to express my sudden terror, but there are too many of them. Even Sue knew to keep quiet, but how she had braved their presence from her room to ours? But, they hadn't stopped her.

They are still, unresponsive to me and, evidently, Sue's journey. I quickly roll over to wake my husband.

I whisper as I shake him. "Jeffrey, wake up!"

He grumbles as he begins to stir. "What is—"

I know he sees. His breath suddenly stops and there is a moment as reaction and thoughtful response fight in his head. He springs to his feet throwing the sheets from himself, but stops himself with a curse under his breath.

The figures make no movements. No shifting their weight or idle cock of one head to see our family was awake now. They remain unnaturally still. There are too many of them to consider rash actions. These figures could close in on us and stop us in our tracks on a whim.

He turns to see us, Sue now holding her finger to her lips.

He asks anyway, "Were they in your room?"

She gives him a quick affirmative nod.

We sleep in little more than our underwear. They stand in front of closet doors and the closed bathroom. No grabbing robes or clothes, but we share an urge to get out of the house, cold winter night be damned. Jeffrey urges us to follow him. As Sue goes around and I slide off the bed, the figures along the walls make no attempts to interrupt our actions. I briefly wonder if I'm having a night terror, but my movements feel solid, like I am in control. He takes my hand, in turn I take Sue's, and we walk down the hall to the living room.

They're everywhere, all the same height, all perfectly still. Is this a practical joke? Could they be mannequins? I almost want to check, to reach out and push one, but the texture of their cloaks and the void of darkness within their hoods makes me rethink the impulse, like they would feel like mold or a slug's skin.

The front door is covered by two figures, no visible sign of any break-in.

Jeffrey speaks calmly, asking me, "Did you do this, is this a joke?"

I feel insulted at first, but he did wake up last. I tell him, "We're as scared as you are."

Jeffrey holds out his free hand, palm down, trying to convey he presented no threat. "Please let us through…" he asks them.

The two figures step aside, making their first movements we've seen. Another robed figure outside of the house opens the door wide, as if knowing exactly when they should, and stepped aside allowing us to exit.

The blast of chilly air hits our exposed bodies, but fear and adrenaline propel us.

Reaching the threshold, I grip Jeffrey's hand tighter. "They're *everywhere*."

The figures appeared to line the street in front of the house. Stepping through the doorway, we can see they've surrounded the house, all shoulder to shoulder, all militantly still.

"Oh my god, they're even in the tree." I said, a cry threatening to choke my throat.

Jeffrey looks up to the leafless oak in our front yard where, somehow, there stands more figures among the branches. Straight and tall, holding nothing for support. A few of them stand at the ends of branches on little more than twigs, impossibly not bending their perches.

Could they be props? Many of them could be fake to contribute to the illusion, it would explain how they were so still… But the thought is broken when one in the tree, standing at the end of a branch that shouldn't support a human's weight, drops to the ground, revealing boots as the robe flares in the descent, and the figure's knees bend under the robe to cushion the impact. There is no sound.

They walk toward us at the open door but stop short of our porch. Raising their right arm, they gesture with a gloved hand for us to return into our house.

Jeffrey takes a single step backward, indicating he understands the command.

The one that opened the door steps back outside, closing the door with them. The other two within the house resume their blockade of the door.

I can sense Jeffrey doing the mental gymnastics to recall if he had indeed locked the doors. It was part of his nightly routine, to check every door was locked, even the cellar door in the kitchen that didn't access the outside. I sense it because I'm thinking it myself.

A rich, deep voice comes from behind us in the kitchen. Despite its depth, I can't identify an accent or gender, "You really shouldn't leave fruit out like this."

We each turned at the sound, Sue gasping. Jeffrey moves himself between us to shield us from this new, talkative figure. I try to keep Sue between the two of us, doing my best to keep us safe from behind.

This one is different from the others. The cloak appears to be yellow in the single light left on over the sink. It's dingy, though, old and moth-eaten. The foot of the cloak looks as though it has waded through all manner of muck and become tattered and frayed, revealing worn, black boots. Where the other figures lining the walls and standing outside all have hoods hanging so low, they hide faces, this one has a smaller, close-fitting hood. However, the face is still concealed by a golden mask of a placid face, its soft edges glittering in the light, the only thing that shines about the figure.

"If you want to decorate," they continue, the mask moving slightly with movement underneath. "I suggest plastic fruits and keep them clean for that 'fresh' look. You attract flies with real fruit."

They hold up an apple in a black glove, examining it. A fly is crawling near the stem. They swipe the pest with their thumb, rub the apple between both hands as if to wipe it clean, but the gloves are sooty and leave black smears on the apple's skin.

The mask's mouth opens, but there isn't a break or hinge. The whole face contorted into what looks like a scream of anger. They turn toward us, and I can see the eyes and mouth are pits. There is nothing behind the mask—no eyes, no open mouth with teeth to bite into the fruit—just darkness that hurts my eyes as much as looking directly at the sun. They bite into the apple, the mask snapping back to its expressionless form. It moved from action behind it, soft crunching the only noise to fill the room.

Jeffrey measures each syllable, asking, "What do you want from us?"

The figure steps to one side and gestures with the hand holding the apple for us to sit at our own table.

We stay still.

The figure shrugs. "I want nothing from *you*, per se, providing you do not get in *my* way. But I do have a favor to ask… I mean you no harm, I assure you. Very much the opposite. Please—sit."

A cordial home invader and an eerie horde. Given what we have seen so far, what else is there to do? I touch Jeffrey's shoulder and he cautiously moves forward with us in tow. In the kitchen, the figures line the counters, blocking access to anything that could possibly be used as a weapon. We are in this—whatever "this" is—and to survive for as long as we can, to protect our daughter, is the only motivation we can consider.

Jeffrey and I quietly pull chairs from the table. Sue drags hers across the floor, causing a cacophony to interrupt the silence. She immediately looks at us with an apology in her face. It's a bad habit we have tried to break her of and now it makes things feel suddenly uncomfortable.

The figure in yellow takes a place at the table and pauses behind the chair. He looks directly at Sue, then dramatically presses down and pulls the chair to make an even louder break in the silence. Sue, despite her fear, or maybe because of it, giggles a little. She quickly silenced, though, when the mask again changed shape into the laughing side of a theater mask. As they sit, the mask shifts back as they take another bite of dirty apple.

They crunch and wave the apple at us. The bite marks look human, but the flesh of the apple looks like it's already browning as if it had sat out too long.

They speak around their mouthful, "I suppose you have questions, which is fair."

Jeffrey speaks through gritted teeth, repeating, "What do you want from us?"

"Ah, come now," they say leaning back. "I already said 'nothing.' I am here—"

"How did so many of you get into our house?" my husband's anger overwhelms him.

The figure leans forward, as if excited to be asked that particular question and in turn responded, "How many brain cells do you have?"

"What?" my husband shakes his head, confused.

"How did you move your mouth just now?" they say, nearly coming out of their seat. "How did you choose that word? Why did you react the way you did?"

Jeffrey stammers.

"It's okay." They relax back into their seat. "There are as many of us as are needed, and we move in the same way that you move your arm; there is no conscious directive. We move where we are needed, when we are needed. You are, unfortunately, caught in the middle. Most of the time we are needed in remote locations, the middle of a field, a deserted stretch of highway, but sometimes it is someone's home; sometimes they are empty, sometimes they are full.

"You are already formulating the question as to how you've never heard of a massive amount of people suddenly showing up and terrifying homes. The Earth is large, larger than people tend to consider. No place is much more than 48 hours away from civilization, but people occupy only about 10% of the Earth's surface. It is very rare indeed that we move within inhabited or noticeable places. You sadly just so happen to sit right on top of where I need to be. Plain bad luck."

"But what are you needed *for*?" Jeffrey demands. "Why here, in our house, in the middle of the night, with these robes and cryptic, cult-y bullshit?"

The mask morphs into the angry scream with too dark pits. Mocking us? They take another bite of the apple and chew as the mask snaps back into place.

"If we're being frank, Jeffrey," they say after swallowing, but before we can inquire how they know my husband's name. "There is something that has been in the Earth since before the planet cooled enough to sustain water and life. It is a dangerous thing that must be kept in check. It proliferates throughout the universe, but right now, it is a monster that has grown underneath your beds. It is indistinguishable from the dirt, rocks, and roots you find if you dig, but it is there. It churns with the movement of the earth. I banish it deeper. But, nothing within the Earth remains buried for long. It moves up through solid stone, spreads with the motion of tectonic plates, grows and thrives in hidden places, sometimes causing no harm, sometimes threatening life as you know it, not that *you* would know it. It exists *to* exist. It will take on whatever life it can grab hold of and make it like itself. It devours and assimilates, and given the chance, it would spread like a fire across the surface of the Earth and turn everything into a living death that simply lies in wait."

I ask them, "For what?"

"For all things to die," they say looking at me, knowing my name, too. "For the sun to expand so it can infect the sun's surface, and some countless millions of years from now, spread out across space when the sun explodes."

Sue chimes in, latching onto something she recognizes. "Like, uh, like fungus!"

"Yes!" they say as the mask shifts into the laughing face again. "You must be a very good student, Sue. Fungus is very similar in its lifecycle. However, what lies below us is conscious, it seeks to expand itself, it is crafty and deceitful, not randomly groping for advantages. It may grow like a fungus, but it is an ancient creature that aims to devour as much of the universe as it can continue to grow."

Jeffrey growls, "How do you know our names?"

"What lies beneath is not the only thing that is eternal, Jeffrey." The laughing mask shifts into the crying side of a theater mask. "As I said, there are as many of us as are needed and we move where we are needed. Knowing the environment we occupy is necessary. Time does not move only forward. It moves in all directions, and I move through it to the places the thing has always been. I am with it always, so I am everywhere as well, for all of time. I seek my lost kingdom and love, destroyed by a creature of death and rot. This moment has always been, we have always had this conversation, and we always keep the thing in its place. And we always will. You and I—Sue."

Jeffrey stood fast, knocking his chair backward and sending it clattering to the floor. It nearly hit one of the figures, where I noticed that they did not even flinch.

"That is enough!" my husband cried. "I don't know how the hell you got in here or what you're really planning to do, but trying to draw us, my *daughter*, into some science fiction horror nonsense is over the line. We don't have to take this cultist shit! I will rip that mechanical mask off your face and shove it down your throat! Overpower me, go ahead! But you are not killing my family without a fight."

The man in yellow leaned back in his chair. The mask was now pallid and expressionless. "Mask? I wear no mask."

Jeffrey started to come around the table when the man stood just as quickly also knocking his chair back, this one actually hitting a figure, though they still did not move or react.

The man in yellow seemed to be much taller now. The solitary light over the sink seemed to dim, but his robe intensified, a burning yellow now, sunlight made into cloth. The face of the mask did not change, but I felt like the eyes were burning holes straight through us.

At once, the man and every figure, even seemingly the ones outside, spoke in unison. "I am not the enemy here. But I will kill you where you stand should you take one step closer. There is a thing that sprouts in your cellar now, a tiny spore, a spec you would not even notice, but breathe it in and you would become death. My killing you would be a mercy."

Jeffrey, Sue, and I looked around in terror as the same voice boomed from every figure. It was impossible to choreograph such a thing. How could those lined along the walls of the bedrooms, the ones outside, know when to speak?

The voice returned to just the man in yellow. "Do I have your attention, then?"

Jeffrey said nothing.

"As many as are needed," the man said. "Moving without thought, unencumbered by time, unlimited by space. I am here, I am there, I am everywhere. And just for your peace of mind…"

He reached up to his face, the mask, and gripped it, pulling at the edges. A sound of flesh tearing and wet popping accompanied the task. Blood began to gush down the front of his robe.

Sue's eyes were streaming tears, my husband stared blankly, and I stammered, unable to comprehend what I was seeing, a deeply unsettling blankness filling my mind. I could not look away if I wanted to. Somehow, we were being forced to watch..

Finally, the mask tore free. Ragged bits of flesh, bright red blood clinging to that painful black, hung from the edges. Nothing was behind the mask, but blood continued to pour down his chest. The man set the mask on the table and leaned forward to stare at the bowl of fruit. The apples, bananas, and oranges began to darken, shrivel, and rapidly decay under the man in yellow's gaze. The bowl even began to age and cracks formed under some unknown pressure. The table groaned and seemed to be buckling in the center.

"Enough!" my husband's voice finally said, breaking free of the spell.

The man in yellow straightened again and deliberately took care not to look at any of us. He raised the mask back to his face. The strips of strange, bloody flesh began to reach into the darkness of the hood like tentacles reaching forth for some unseen anchor within. The blood along his front glistened in the single light, yet somehow, none had fallen to the table, not even where he had set the mask.

With the mask returned, I felt completely freed and looked down at the table. The fruit, bowl, and table were all fine, but the emotional reaction of my daughter and husband were real, their faces red and wet from tears and the shock of what had just happened. It felt like being crushed along with the table while the man's mask was removed.

"How does *that* give me 'peace of mind'?" my husband wheezed.

"It is the method by which I will rid your home of this menace."

Jeffrey had to force himself to breathe. "And why do you need my daughter?"

"Innocence." Sue said. She seemed to be very far away and privy to something we were not. "Youth. A life unlived. I'll attract it."

"The wisdom of a child never ceases to amaze." The man said.

Jeffrey knelt next to Sue, despite being a young teen, she seemed so very small in this moment. "You don't have to do anything you don't want to, I'll protect you."

Sue looked at him, tears in her eyes. "You can't protect me from that." She said looking at the fruit on the table.

Kneeling opposite Jeffrey, the man also implored Sue. "I have frightened you, and for that I am sorry. But, you are correct. The thing within the earth will be most attracted to you. It is only by chance that it has risen here, but you would be the best host in this place, and because of that, I would very much appreciate your help."

"You want to use my daughter as bait." Jeffrey stated as though he had accepted it.

"Please," I said from across the table. "Clearly you can handle such a thing by yourself."

"I will not lie," the man said. "You are correct. I could bury it further down and it could be days, weeks, *years* before it reappeared somewhere else. But if I can get it to reveal itself, I can crush it, and bury it so much deeper."

He turned back to Sue. "It will not be easy. The task itself is simple: stand still. But what you will see, what you will hear, will change you. You will help me protect the whole world and countless people. Will you do this willingly?"

Sue nodded without hesitation, but tears had begun to roll down her cheeks again.

"Then let it be done." He said and stood, offering his hand to her.

She stood and took it, and they took the few steps to the cellar door together. The door opened with neither of them reaching for it, more figures along the walls to the cellar. The door shut behind them and there was the distant sound of the man's boots on each step, slow as Sue padded beside him.

Jeffrey stood and two figures filled in the gap to the door. He went to the other side of the table to put his hands on my shoulders as we waited. We never heard Sue make a sound, but the man, and the figures, all hummed some sort of chant and we could feel vibrations in the floor. Just below us, *something* was happening. A sound of scuffling, earth shifting, the sound of wood bending to the point of breaking. The man in yellow must have removed his mask again as a groan of what sounded like a house settling, a subtle moan followed by loud pops began to issue from below.

A cry sounded, something in astounding pain, but not Sue or the man, no human could make such a sound. A bang like gunshot reported and shook the entire house. Another unearthly cry, this time of anger, frustration. All the while, neither Sue or the man made a sound. Something thrashed, items crashed, and something was crushed under intense weight; the gaze of the man in yellow.

Then they were gone. The figures along the walls disappeared and the house was silent again. There was no sound along with it, it did not happen between blinks, they very simply vanished.

Jeffrey and I rushed for the cellar door. Upon flinging it open, Sue was already halfway up the stairs. We could tell she was pale even in the darkness, her skin looked ashen and her face was somewhere between horrified and exhausted. She climbed the rest of the way up then shouldered past us and walked steadily toward her room.

We followed her, watched her crawl robotically into bed, her back to us.

"Sue, sweetheart," I began.

127

Sue did not move. "Never ask."

FAR AWAY

ATG

"Sir?" Communications called to the overnight Commander. "Uh, there seems to be an issue…"

The Commander responded by stepping up behind Communications to look over her shoulder.

"The emergency band just opened." She continued. "We pinged the signal coming from the IPF Tano, but no distress signal was actually sent. Now we're unable to establish the security-handshake, despite the ship is still there. It's just—*silent.*"

Coms could hear the Commander stiffen and sigh. "That shouldn't be possible…"

"Of course, Sir. We're still waiting on a response from Earth to see if they can make contact. That will be a few minutes. I wanted to bring it to your attention before they hailed. The Tano is in line of sight, we've pinged them with every method, even the emergency band, but the only thing we get back is that the ship is intact, there, and still moving toward us."

"The ship's systems should still respond to the handshake, though." The Commander said mostly to himself. "That's not a part of their communications, it's tied to the blackbox for just such emergencies—"

"Yes, Sir," Communications dared to interrupt, "Destruction would make more sense, but we can see it, the ship should respond, yet…"

The Commander didn't move; rather, he straightened and addressed the bridge, "Can we pull up that visual on the Tano, please?"

A field of stars filled the main display. A blue ring surrounded a dot hardly distinguishable from any other star across the backdrop.

"This is the Tano," Coms said. "Until the incident, it was responding to route checks from both us and Earth at the regularly scheduled intervals. Telemetry indicates it's still en route, no change in speed or course... There are no known obstacles along its course, no solar activity in the vicinity, and even if there were an actual accident of *any* type, the handshake would have notified us. Even the emergency band should have had a system status report upon opening. The Tano is essentially a rock in space at this point. I don't want to say it, Sir, but, I don't know what to do."

The Commander shifted his weight, and Coms could hear him take a few calming breaths. "Captain won't be happy, but I'll wake her."

❧❦

The Communications officer had spent a lot of time in her youth and military career in low gravity between Mars and the simulated gravity of military transports and space stations, giving her significant height over the Captain. The Captain, an Earthling toward the end of her career, still yet retained a youthful, confident presence that intimidated younger "space born" crew. The Captain was sure to catch Communication's eye as she passed to take her seat on the bridge and gave her curt acknowledgment.

"Earth has reported that the Interplanetary Freighter ship 'Tano' is silent to them, as well," Coms said as the rest of the crew returned to their stations. She swallowed hard despite a dry mouth. "They report that no unusual activity preceded the silent emergency band blip. They are preparing a Hawking kite-probe; we should have a better visual on the Tano in sixteen hours. At current, launching a Rescue/Retrieval/Salvage from Earth would take longer than for the Tano to reach us at its present clip. Mounting an RRS from the COAX should be contingent upon the kite's findings, per Earth, Sir."

Coms stood stock still, awaiting the Captain's response.

The "at ease" she finally gave sounded as though something in the back of her throat growled it out through her mouth, rather than speaking for herself. But, Coms was thankful, regardless, and gave a curt bow of her head, resuming her station.

The Captain stared at the ring of blue highlighting the Tano. At a hundred million miles away, it was as insignificant and silent against the backdrop as a mote of dust. The Tano was bringing supplies to the Ceres Orbiting Ancillary Exchange and points beyond. At this time of year, Mars was too far away, so no rescue mission from there, either. The Tano was barely closer to Ceres than to anything else and approaching as otherwise expected. It would still be a month before it arrived. If it came to it, launching a ship from the COAX would take half that time.

The Captain looked at the overnight Commander. "Considering our options are waiting and hurrying up *to* wait, you could have sent a priority missive apprising me of the situation."

The Commander bowed, but did not apologize.

Sighing, the Captain said, "See if we can't rustle a better image of the Tano in the meantime. Set all communication methods on an urgent loop requesting immediate reply, both from their ship and coms. Keep an eye out for alternative communication methods from the ship; they may need to be thinking creatively, and so do we.

"Commander, this is *indeed* an urgent matter—I appreciate being notified; however, with Earth saying to wait for the kite probe's details, there's nothing *we* can do *right now*. A rested chain of command is a more effective one."

"Yes, Captain."

The Captain stood and strode off almost silently, but paused in the doorway. "Commander… please alert me immediately if there is *any* change in this situation."

The Commander bowed, "Of course, Captain."

੭੦੬

The bridge was bustling. No one from the night crew had left when their morning relief came. The Captain was patient and allowed the spectators, so long as they weren't in the way and were willing to lend their skills where possible. The COAX wasn't outfitted with powerful telescopes, so their imaging was hardly improved. However, they watched a feed from the Hawking kite. Pushed by a solar system wide laser array, it zoomed toward the Tano much faster than a manned craft could achieve.

Outwardly, the Tano looked normal—bulky cargo blocks forming a cylinder under a mile in length. The ship *itself* was basically a tugboat at the front of the crates. It would be another hour before the probe came alongside the Tano-proper. Despite the visual confirmation of the ship, the probe was unable to establish a communication link, either.

Someone said, "What was that?" before the visual cut out. There were laughs and groans of frustration, but they were quick to silence as the Captain stood.

"Get a report from Earth, corroborate anything we find in the minutes leading up to the loss of the feed." The Captain barked. She turned toward the person who had spoke before the transmission broke. "What did you see?"

"Uh…" The ensign shifted in his boots, but gained his composure quickly. "It was like a shimmer, like, the surface of the crates were sparkling. Not icy, though, prismatic… Captain."

"Agreed." The Captain said. "I want everyone in here to report their personal accounts of the Tano in the last hour. Everyone has access to the recorded feed, I want as much detail as you can supply. And don't look at just the ship. Take in the surroundings; every pixel of the kite's feed needs to have an eyeball on it. Something is disrupting communications around the Tano, and we need to find out *what* before it reaches us. It's going to be a while before Earth responds and longer still before they have any information, so let's clear the bridge. I need everyone rested and alert."

There was no hesitation. The off-duty crew dispersed, and barely another word was spoken.

❧⟡❧

Earth had no answers; their feed did not have any more to offer despite the benefit of a direct contact through the laser array. Both they and the COAX could pick up the kite itself, perfectly intact, now *silent*. The probe had been set to sidle along the Tano's cargo and settle near the crew module. Visually, it appeared the probe had continued to follow its program, so that indicated whatever silencing bubble surrounded the ship didn't affect mechanical workings. It was entirely possible the Tano was as concerned with the silence from the COAX and Earth.

After pouring over the footage, crew reports were consistent, but yielded little. The freight containers shimmered as if coated in a fine frost; yet, none of those containers, nor the ship itself, had ever been within Earth's atmosphere, so moisture shouldn't have collected on those surfaces. Nor was there any comet debris it would have passed through along its route.

A minimum safe distance was calculated, decently outside of where the initial probe lost communication, and Earth fired off a modified Hawking kite with a more powerful camera. The hope was that they could orbit outside the assumed sphere of silence and peer into the Tano's portholes to determine the crew's safety. It would be several more hours before they started gleaning any new information.

Space, being so vast and empty, made for a lot of waiting around. It had been two whole days since the Tano went silent. Six shift changes. Two people used sick time, and four people had to work extra hours to fill the gap. Mostly, working the command module of the COAX was as boring as waiting for things to happen in space. But, the mystery of the Tano had captured everyone's attention, and if they weren't legitimately working, they were watching either the first probe's recording or waiting for the feed to start on the second.

The Captain didn't mind. The nightshift Commander didn't mind. When the flashing started, however, almost everyone crowded the Communications workstation.

"Is it Morse code?"

"No, the bursts are too long…"

"Forward jets?"

"Too bright…"

"…and it's not losing speed."

"Fire on their bridge?"

"I hope not!"

"That's still too bright."

"It's dying out at random."

"*Someone's* trying to communicate, they have to be."

That was the hope, but they wouldn't know for a few hours more.

The overnight Commander considered waking the Captain again, but calculated that the probe would be transmitting the pertinent information as the Captain took the bridge. Best to let her sleep, but he sent a priority message to her anyway.

"Sir?" Communications said. "I think it's on the outside of the Tano; it might be a laser tool."

"Are they just trying to get our attention? 'Hey, we're here'?"

"I can't be certain, but I don't think they're pointing it at us—I think…"

"What is it?"

Coms sighed. "I think someone is writing on the outside of the ship. The flashes could correspond to someone writing large letters."

The gathered crew began to speculate on what that could mean. It seemed like a drastic maneuver, considering the crew of the Tano should have noticed the first Hawking kite.

It would be another ten days before the COAX's own scopes could really make out any detail of the Tano. The ship was still twenty-five days out from meeting the COAX. In a few hours, they would learn if Communications was onto something.

The Commander sent another priority message.

DO NOT DOCK
DO NOT BOARD
DUST CLOUD 10 DAYS OUT
CREW WENT MAD
NOTHING BUT SCREAMING
I'M DEAF WHAT I SAW
GLAD TO DIE IN SILENCE

When the second probe rounded the Tano and took in the message etched into the hull, the crew of the COAX were stunned into their own otherworldly silence. The body of a crewman was tethered to the ship and dangling. The torch they had used to burn the message for the COAX to see before it was "too late" was tethered to them, though

135

dangling as helplessly. EVA suits only had so much atmosphere and this individual let themselves expire rather than go back inside.

The Captain cleared the bridge of all but essential crew. There was no protest, though this time, there did seem to be an urgency to exit. Whatever else they discovered from here was certain to be unsettling.

The Lieutenant Commander chimed in. "We have confirmation of an Ezekiel Jansen on the crew manifest—he's hearing impaired, Captain."

"What do we have on this Ezekiel Jansen?" the Captain asked.

"Commendable," the Lt. Commander said, reading from a dossier. "No military experience, but he's been contracted for deep space missions like this for about five years, serving as engineering crew. He's made employee of the month several times… If whatever affected the crew operates on the auditory senses, he may have been immune, even considering, or because of, his cochlear implant."

The Captain thanked them. Quick and creative thinking was what she needed right now. They were facing an unknown situation with a nightmarish scenario playing out millions of miles away.

"Any indication he could mutiny and sabotage ship systems?" The Captain asked. "Are we willing to accept a mysterious extraterrestrial *contagion*?"

The Lt. Commander thumbed an invisible document in front of him. "He's a good kid. Maybe mass hysteria after encountering the unidentified debris? There were six aboard, counting him. He'd served with all of them before; this is his third trip to the COAX and second aboard the Tano. Whatever happened, he has tried to warn us. We still have a few weeks before it would arrive; we should be able to divert it and bring it to a halt before that bubble of silence reaches us. We might not be able to communicate with probes, but controlled, preprogrammed tug-bots could do the job."

"How many bots would we need to sacrifice?" the Captain asked. "I don't think we want to risk reclaiming anything until we have a firm understanding of what is going on."

The Lt. Commander did some calculations. "Six, maybe. Two to disengage thrusters, two to divert, two to decelerate, each on dedicated tasks in case cascading function commands fail within the bubble."

"How can we deal with the possibility the Tano wouldn't defend itself? We're not certain on the condition of the crew aboard the ship, or if the ship has emergency protocols engaged to deflect foreign objects."

The crew sat quiet for a moment.

The Security Chief suggested, "Controlled demolition? If this dust cloud ruined their communications and somehow affected the crew, should we even risk any of it reaching the COAX? It should be treated as a liability and potential threat."

The Captain frowned. "I concur; however, we have a duty to Jansen and his crew to learn what happened here. Let's get on the same page with Earth. We want to park the Tano off the shipping lanes and study it from afar. But a full-stop implosion demolition may be necessary."

"Captain," the Communications officer called. "You're going to want to see this."

Without waiting for the order, Coms placed the live feed from the second probe on the main display. In the portholes were the faces of the rest of the Tano's crew. But, *only* their faces.

Like paper-mâché masks hung in the windows of a schoolroom, the five skinned faces filled portholes, gruesomely warning that only carnage lay within. More disturbing still, the crew members appeared to still be milling about the ship. Their skull faces locked in eternal screams. Lips and eyelids removed, there was no shutting out the horror. Their ears were scratched away, yet a bloody hand would still reach to attempt to block or claw away whatever had driven them here.

The Captain couldn't decide on an expression to wear in response to the hideous image, but someone on the bridge, sounding very far away, excused themselves in a hurry.

"Turn it off."

It wasn't the Captain's order—it wasn't clear who said it—but Coms complied anyway. The Captain didn't argue.

"Destroy it," the Captain finally breathed.

137

"Captain, I understand emotions might be running high," the Commander countered, "but as you said, we owe it to the crew. If there's a *chance* we could help them—"

Without turning to face the Commander or any other crew member, the Captain seethed. "That thing has destroyed six lives and silenced machinery. Machinery with so much redundancy we should be able to ping it with *sonar* in the vacuum of space and get a 'hello' back, but we can't confirm its status beyond the fact it's *there*. It silenced a probe that didn't even come into contact. I will not endanger this crew—"

"Captain—" Coms interrupted. "Um, Captain, the wide spectrum emergency broadcast channel from Earth just opened then immediately closed—Earth is silent."

Gasps severed the air like a paper cut.

The Captain whispered, "Destroy it."

I WOKE UP.DOCU

ATG

I woke up because I could hear you snoring. It's three a.m. and I'm wide awake now. Odd that the things which once annoyed us become the things we miss. I miss sleeping beside you. Or, at least, I miss lying beside you and listening to you snore. But, I understand that's not an option anymore. It's three a.m. and I'm all alone, wide awake, with no one to talk to but this computer screen.

I remember the last time we slept together. We made love. It was slow and deliberate. We tried to prolong it as long as we could, like we knew it was the last time. Maybe you did. You kissed me, I held you, and when I woke up, you weren't there.

It's been a struggle ever since. To hold on to that memory, the sounds, smells. I fret when your face is gone, or the sound of your voice. These fleeting memories are a curse and I grasp and claw at them. I force myself to replay them in my mind, over and over, when I can catch them. They slip, though, and I worry if they'll ever come back.

I remember everything right now, though. Even the lost moments. It's all here, like there was never a problem. Something about your snore clicked everything into place. The moments of clarity are few and far between now, I know, and too short. That's why I'm writing this down. That's why I didn't wake you. I couldn't risk losing it, I have things to say.

Right now I can recall times that we were talking and I would slip away, replaced by a blank slate completely unaware of our ongoing conversation. It was still me, but like a reset button has been pressed. I have to recollect the data. I know in the moment that I've lost something, it's painful. I feel embarrassed and ashamed, but you're only ever kind and start over with me. I want to cry when it happens…but sometimes the reason why eludes me. So when I'm a blubbering mess for seemingly no reason, the reason is regret, only I can't express it.

I know it's hard on you, your emotions and patience. I've seen the look of frustration flash in your eyes, followed by pity and that smile. Even though you're faking it, it's still so warm. I know it's hardest when I don't recognize your face and even resist you. Those are scary for me, too. Imagine feeling a new pain throughout your body you can't explain and no one can help you. I have entire days like that, except I know what the pain is: it's me being erased from my own body. The shell of me is desperately trying to protect what little is left. If…*when* I lash out at you, I'm sorry; I'm physically fighting an internal struggle.

I know you're lonely. I know you've been staying at work late to see friends. I know you've gone on dates. There have been times I've heard you on the phone. I suspect you suspect I suspect. And it's okay. I approve. I'm all but gone these days. The last *conversation* we held at length has probably been a month ago. It's been flashes of recognition, jabs of old jokes, and smiles in quiet times. I've been stuck in the backseat of my brain for a long time. You need a companion, not a charge.

I wish I could tell you I'm in here all the time, looking out at you, that you could talk to me and I would absorb it all. It's more like I'm sleepwalking at all hours of the day and night; a bit of a memory will come back, something I say will make sense to you as I say it, but I won't recall it till much later, even though *I* said it. That's why I repeat myself so much. I'm sorry for that, too. I can hear the annoyance in your voice when I've said the same thing for a third time, for the third day in a row.

One of the worst feelings, in these moments of clarity, is realizing our daughter and her children are afraid of me. I can't blame them. I will think that she is you, or that they're intruders, or I think they're her and her friends and I never get the names right. I know when I struck the boy…that was the last straw. I regret it, but it was a blank version of me, closer to a toddler than a grandparent. It's no excuse. I

141

know that they don't hate me. They're just protecting themselves from a potential threat, as they should. But I miss them, when I remember.

I'm slowing down, struggling. I can feel the broken bits trying to reclaim their territory in my brain. I'm trying to hold onto this moment, to finish it properly, like when we made love. Like then, it feels like this might be the last. I feel like I've been given time— finite— to say my goodbyes. I know when you read this, when you share it with the family, you'll try to show me and ask me to remember. That will only upset me; partly because I will, but not exactly. That shame consumes the flashes and reflections of me that can't hold the pieces together. I feel like a failure, but I *know* I'm not.

I'm writing this, ultimately, to tell you and our family, that I love you. I might be confused and lost, but I appreciate everything you've done for me. I've had a life worth living because of *you*. If it's time for you to move on, know that I am okay. If I need to be in a place that is better suited to care for my needs, all I ask is that you come see me when you can. I'm sure medicines can keep me calm so even the grandkids can come. When you do come, if you come, I'll try to wave and say hi from the backseat here in my brain.

I love you and thank you for loving me.

❧

Nurse Morris printed off the letter and put it with the others. It was essentially the same every time, but every time it made her cry. She stood from the nurse's station, forced a yawn and wiped away the burgeoning tears. With a few gulps and a sigh, she straightened and smoothed her smock before heading down the hall.

He was asleep, his breath long and deep, threatening to shatter into a cacophonous snore. He hadn't even stirred when the door clicked open. She touched his shoulder and his breathing stopped. Startled, he finally let out his breath in a growl. He liked sleeping in, but he would grumble even more if he did. He groaned and slid up to sit. There was a look of remorse in his face.

"I saw your letter, Carter." Nurse Morris said.

He looked at her, questioning at first, then confused as he searched for a meaning or response, then his eyes lit up, like they did. "Can you make sure Alex gets it?"

No matter how many times it happened, it was hard. "Now, Carter, you have to try to *remember*."

He slouched, looking down at the blanket covering his lap. She knew he knew, but sometimes the cobwebs had to be blown out. He began to nod.

"Three years now." He said with a heave.

She pulled the chair against the wall over to the side of the bed. "Carter, we've talked about this. You've got to stop breaking into our computers. I know you wake up in the middle of the night and you can get confused—"

"But you don't want me fouling up the works."

She put her hand on his knee. "We have to change our passwords all the time, thanks to you. I'm not sure how you do it, you resourceful old man."

"Don't make passwords from stuff on your desk…" he trailed off.

"Are you okay?" she asked after a moment. "Do you want to come to the common room and have breakfast?"

He continued to stare at his lap.

"Carter?" she asked.

He looked up, sullen.

She frowned.

He smiled. "Nurse Morris! Good morning!"

She patted his knee. "C'mon, Carter, time for breakfast."

He started to say something, but stopped with his mouth in mid-formation. He sighed. "I suppose it's better to think they're still around every so often, right? To have that glimmer of hope…that makes me sound pathetic."

"You are not *pathetic*, Carter." Nurse Morris said sharply. "Sometimes family goes before us, we just have to remember them…"

She felt a pang of regret for her choice of words.

His eyes slid to stare her down through his periphery, but he shook it off. "I suppose I do keep them alive in my own way if I'm stuck in the past with them."

"There you go." Nurse Morris said approvingly. "Find the positive in all things."

He swung his legs over the side of the bed, the tendons and veins in his feet flexing and sliding as he wiggled his toes. "When did I get so old?"

"You're only as old as you feel." She said, offering a hand to help him up.

"I feel a thousand."

She chuckled.

"Is there waffles this morning?"

"There's always waffles, Carter."

He shook his head. "I hate waffles."

"I know you do, Carter."

THE LAST TREE

ST

Down in the village, they tell the children not to go past the tree-line, the open scrubland is dangerous. Everything, even predators, stay in the forest. To venture out into that empty expanse at the foot of the mountain, with no place to hide, is to invite all manner of beasts. So, the children are told to keep safe by the adults, but they tell each other a monster is out there beyond the trees. Children grow and eventually have children of their own, and the warning with the legend grows with them. A dying thing lies in wait for those who dare travel past the forest, and dying things are best left alone.

No one knows what it looks like, though they know exactly where it lives: at the base of a cleaved rockface, where one tree grows much higher up than the rest of the forest. It is the *last tree*, a marker for where forested, rolling hills end, and rocky, unforgiving mountains begin. The field below the cliff is strewn with grey rocks and mud, a trickle of water feeding a quagmire where moss, sickly shrubs, and the last tree grows. Rodents, insects, and birds flit between rocks and clumps. Otherwise it's a desolate expanse no good for climbing the mountain or foraging for resources. The monster lives *there*, only barely—so the children say—to stay alone, away from the village, away from the world, waiting to die. Its only company also its home, the twisted and gangly tree pushing higher up than any other thing growing there.

The first one rests at the tree-line, stopping at an invisible line drilled into their memory as the place to go no further. The second one is strapped to a sledge, immobile. They stare out over the slope, up to the last tree, up to the mountain. The first one shifts their weight and drags the second one along, stepping out of scrubland into gravel and mud. There will be no turning back now.

"So, you're going to do it, huh?" the second one says.

The first one keeps moving.

"Remember when we would dare each other to do this? '*Run up to the last tree and back again as fast as you can!*' we would cry, shouting in excitement the whole way. Those were good times, weren't they?"

The first one doesn't respond. They continue through the muck.

"Who did it that one time?"

Still, silence.

"I can start singing again…" the second one lilts.

"Pascal." The first one begrudgingly barks.

"That's right! Whatever happened to Pascal?"

"Moved away."

"Nah, Pascal didn't move away. That's just what the grown-ups said to keep us from asking questions. Pascal got gobbled up."

The first one huffs.

"Gobbled up by the last tree. We all saw it. That's how we know to stay away. But, here we are."

They're nearly to the tree when the first one stops. The second one is heavy and a bother.

"You can't stop now."

"Pascal wasn't eaten." The first one says through panting breaths. "Pascal didn't move away."

"Then what happened to Pascal?"

"Pascal wasn't real. We all share the story, daring each other to touch the last tree. There's always the one who does, and no one knows what happened to them after."

"Pretty sure I remember Pascal. Short, red hair, fast as the wind, though."

"You didn't remember Pascal until I said the name."

"Oh…"

"Come on…"

"I don't think I have much choice."

"You don't. I was talking to myself."

The first one takes the last few steps, dragging the second one to the trunk of the old yellow tree. It's never been green, but never sheds, either, lingering just above death, just above the forest.

The first one sets to unfastening the second one from the sledge and tying them to the tree. The second one doesn't move or say anything, maybe resigned to their fate.

Wind blows down from the mountain, cascading down from some other land they've never known. The tree sways a bit, creaking and groaning in protest. It's earned its place here, standing firm against wind and cold and thinner air. The two are disturbing the last tree's majestic reign over the forest. Somewhere below, a bird cries out.

The second one broaches the silence between them. "How did we end up here?" Their sullen voice breaking through the quiet.

"I brought you through the forest."

They scoff. "I mean it. What are we doing here? What is it you hope to achieve? Am I really a problem you think you can solve with old fairy tales?"

"You're sick." The first one says, shifting to one side to dig something from a pocket. "You're sick and I've brought you here to make sure you'll always be better."

The first one unwraps some dried food and slips it between their hood and scarf.

"Tying me to a tree on a mountainside in the cold won't make me better. Give me some of that whatever it is you're eating—"

"You know you can't eat this." The first one says around a mouthful.

"Because I'm *sick*? Or—"

"Stop!" The first one snaps. "I brought you here so you can get better, so that you'll always be better," they say, quieter.

"Now you're repeating yourself. What does that mean? How can I 'always be better'?"

The first one rewraps their snack and stows it away as they stand. "We're here for you. You need to get better. If you get better, then I'll be better, and if we're both better, then no one needs to know you were ever sick."

"What am I even sick with? How am I sick? What good does bringing me out here do?"

"So that you can get better!" The first one growls. "I just want— *need*—you to be better. No one knows you're sick, so I brought you here. When you're *better*, we can go home, and no one needs to know."

"The elders say to *leave* your problems here. It's so you can forget about them, not to make them different or *better*, whatever that means."

"I can't go back without you. Then they'll know."

"Know what? That I'm *sick*? That you came out here against everyone's warnings? Or that you—"

"Shh!" the first one hisses but says nothing more.

They've begun to wear a groove in the soft, grey mud. The second one remains motionless. The sun, hidden behind a slate of clouds, has begun to set, pitting the surrounding forest and mountains into darkened shadows.

Walking off, the first one begins to pick up sticks and dead clumps of grass. The second one does not call out or struggle in their solitude. When the first one comes back with a bundle of dried detritus to start a fire, the second one resumes their line of questioning.

"What do you think the tree can do for me? Or is it the air? Do you think I'll really get *better*?"

The first one works at starting the fire.

"Okay, tell me how we got here."

"Now who's repeating themselves?"

"I really don't remember—help me."

A stone loosens somewhere up on the mountain and noisily bounces down to join the gravel. The first one looks tentatively up the rockface, but there is nothing there, save cold grey stone against a cold grey sky.

"You don't remember," the first one concedes, "because you've been in and out. And I brought you here because of that. As kids, we're told to stay in the forest because going out into the open makes you an easy target. Simple, common sense stuff. But legends come from somewhere and I've got no other choice."

"The dying thing? You think the myth of a monster that is forever dying that eats anything that comes near is the answer?"

"Not *anything*. Not *everything*. It only eats other things that are *dying*."

"You think I'm dying?"

"You're *not* well."

"You plan to feed me to a dying monster. *That's* how you're going to save me?"

"Of course not! The legend must have some basis in truth. Dying things come to the last tree, but there are no corpses here, no bones. And don't say scavengers! People have seen it, seen sickly animals come to the last tree to die, only to walk right back into the forest, healthy and vibrant as the days of their youth."

"*People have seen it*? Like Pascal?"

The first one scoffs. "There's something about the tree. Healing properties, like herbs."

"Then why am I tied to the tree? Why not let me pick at the branches or roots?"

"If I let you go, you'll run away."

"Why would I run?"

"Because you already tried; when you first got sick."

"I don't remember—"

The first one removes their own hood, revealing a tired face, too old to be young, too young to be old, certainly weary from the ordeal. They sit in silence and stare at each other a long while.

"The whole village was beset, maybe an ill trader came through, or it was in the food stores, but people started getting sick. With the sickness came lethargy, at first, then fright, screaming madness at seemingly nothing, then violence—my god, such terrible things."

The first one nearly chokes on a sob. "If the sickness didn't take you, then the sick one would. To survive was no assurance, scratched or bitten…a death sentence; either by the sickness, with time, or condemned by the village. Madness spread faster than the illness, houses burned down, people struck down in the street for little more than a cough that didn't sound *right*.

"When you showed signs, small as they were…when you didn't get up in the mornings, I knew it was only a matter of time before someone passed judgement. I tried to keep you safe, pretended everything was fine, hoped against hope…but then the screaming started."

The second one makes no sound. Darkness has engulfed the forest below. The meager fire casts the tree in a long, shifting shadow up the cliff. Even in the night, the larger members of the forest steer clear of the region, despite the attraction of the fire. Still yet, eyes are on them, everything moves in a slow dance of anticipation.

Tears cut rivulets into the dirt on the first one's cheeks. They wipe an arm across their face and stare into the flames. "So, I tried to keep you quiet, for your safety. I covered your mouth and tried to keep you calm, but you didn't see me, you saw something else, *not* me. I covered your eyes so you might not see it anymore, but you were so terrified. You shook and wrestled, surely someone outside would hear, and that made me think, 'maybe you hear something…' so I covered your ears. I covered your whole head, like a parent shields their child from their own senses when they are frightened…

"I silenced your screams, I closed your eyes and ears, and I held you still until—" they rub their face vigorously, trying to regain their composure. "I brought you here so that you could get better. If it's a medicine in the last tree, or a monster that eats sickness, I don't care, I'll do anything to make you better, because it was an accident, I didn't mean to—"

The first one's voice hitches in their throat, changing suddenly, the sound of sobbing no longer there.

"Kill me." The first one says in the second one's voice.

And there it is, the truth laid bare. I turn my attention to them now, moving slowly as my skin, thick bark, has stiffened with time.

The first one splutters, disbelieving. They did not expect this. And why would they?

I shake dust from my gnarled branches, loosening into tendrils to feel for the second one tied to my trunk. Dead, a thing for the insects to feast upon; no use for me. I rip the leather cords and examine its body. They have not only been smothered, but the eyes have been gouged into bloody pits, the ears scratched beyond recognition.

I have not spoken in so long, finding a voice is difficult, but something within releases into the air. "That one was not sick," I say and toss the body aside for the scavengers to enjoy.

"What—what—what—"

"You, however," I taste the air with the budding foliage along my trunk and many branching arms. "You are deliciously diseased."

"What—what—what—"

"*The dying thing*," I say, "the *last tree*, a demon of the elder world. Whatever you like. That is '*what—what—what.*'"

The first one finally succumbs to the compulsion to run. They are barely on their feet when I catch them with a root thrust from underground. They scream in panic, but the cry for help echoes uselessly through the forest, bounces up and down the cliff with no one to come to their aid. I rise from the earth, no recognizable creature, a tree made of worms and fungus.

"You were *right* about something, though," I offer, "the dying come to me only to return to their worlds as lively as ever. That, my friend—my *child*—is because I go *with* them."

The root has wrapped around them almost completely, constricting them into immobility—just as they had done to their companion. I squeeze until they can no longer draw breath. Their features darken as blood threatens to burst from their skin like a swollen tick. They gawp like a fish, but no air rushes in. Instead, I deliver a seed, forcing my tendril deep into their throat, planting it in the wall of their gut. Then, I let go, dropping them to the ground with a wet thud.

They heave and cough and wretch but hear me all the same as I am now inside them.

"Go back to your village and tell them the last tree is a safe place for children to play; that the mountains cannot be tamed by fear; that only through perseverance will we grow into the world. The dying thing has gone and the last tree is *good*. Do this, and your sickness will be cured, the sickness in the village will burn itself out. No more screams, now. No more loneliness. No more waiting to die."

ABOUT THE AUTHOR

J.D. Buffington lives in Tulsa, Oklahoma with his wife, daughter, a capricious cat and two devious dogs. He seamlessly weaves vivid nightmares and haunting anxiety together to immerse readers into a state of fright and wonder. He can be found at <u>jdbuffington.com</u>.

MORE BY J.D. BUFFINGTON

41: An Autobiography (Anuci Press)
Fruitless Bodies: A Collection
Come Hither No Malice
In the House of In Between (Velox Books)
The Light Across the Street
Red Clouds